Moon People

by

John Dabell

**Grosvenor House
Publishing Limited**

This book is published by
Grosvenor House Publishing Ltd
28-30 High Street, Guildford, Surrey, GU1 3HY.
www.grosvenorhousepublishing.co.uk

A CIP record for this book
is available from the British Library

ISBN 978-1-908105-66-0

DEDICATION

For Maisy – Love Daddy xxx

Moon People by John Dabell
Front and back covers illustrated by Vincent Vigla

This book is inspired by the works of the
Syrian satirist, Lucian of Samosata.

CONTENTS

WELCOME TO THE MOON

If you are thinking about coming to the moon, then don't. That is, don't just think about it – actually make the effort and come here.

You see, the moon is one of those places you've looked at countless times before and you think you know it. But you don't, really.

For years, seemingly intelligent Earth people believed that nothing lived on the moon. But then again, these are the same people that also thought the Earth was flat.

If you look into your telescope for long enough, then you might just see us – the moon people.

The moon's emergence as one of the solar system's leading visitor attractions has come as a surprise to many – but not to us.

Most educated people think the moon has no atmosphere, which is nonsense. It has a great atmosphere, which is why so many people visit it.

Before you start packing, though, we recommend that you get to know us and our home a little first. This book will help you do just that.

Find out more about what we eat, what music we like, what we do in our spare time, what weather to expect, and how to behave when you get here. You will find plenty more on top of that, too.

Book your stay with us soon. We'll be over the moon to see you. What on Earth are you waiting for?

The Moon People

QUICK FACTS ABOUT THE MOON

Below, we have listed a few facts you may or may not know about the moon. We can make no guarantee as to the accuracy of the data.

Topic	Data
Distance from the Earth	About 9 years if you walked non-stop
Length of day	Depends what time you go to bed
Diameter	Yes, we have one
Weight	Overweight but not morbidly obese
Number of McDonald's	Zero
Winds	Avoid Zones 54 and 68
Gravity	Everywhere except in Zone 40, 40A and 40B
Moons	13 moonlets, called The Baker's Dozen
Number of golf balls found on the moon	197 million
Rings	Available in jewellery stores everywhere
Atmosphere	Great bordering on awesome
Distance from the Immortal Galaxy	10 million billion trillion quadrillion kallumptons
Temperature	Between 40-400 Gum Pips
Exports	Ideas, dreams, diamonds, gudge, fizz bins, books
Imports	Teabags, gasbags, handbags, ragbags and sagbags.
Currency	Goodwill
Religion	Universal
Official language	Lunese
Population	Eccentric, friendly, intelligent, remarkable, shy
Website	www.moonpeople.co.uk

Dictionaries from the Earth and other planets vary in their descriptions of the moon a great deal. There are huge differences and some paint a better picture than others. See what you think and make up your own mind.

Earth dictionaries

Moon – an airless, lifeless, bone-dry ball of nothingness. Not much to do here apart from leave.

The Bridge Dictionary of Stuff

Moon - a desolate and quiet place. Has no water, no souvenirs and the weather is awful. Has a heavily crated surface full of old verrucae. Don't bother.

The Tell It Like It Is Dictionary of Things

Moon – the fifth largest satellite in the solar system and the brightest object in the sky after the sun. But that's about it.

Filbert's Definitive English Dictionary

Moon – a land of cheesy mountains, naff valleys and cheap craters. Not a place for writing home about and would be a wasted journey unless you like dust and silence.

The Bunberry Dictionary of English

Dictionaries around the solar system

The moon is Earth's closest neighbour. This vibrant and dynamic destination is bursting with life and it is the number 1 tourist destination in the solar system. The craters are brilliant for skateboarding.

The Venus Dictionary of Inner Planets and Other Space Stuff Like That

The moon is a magical orb of wondrous wonderment located just off Earth. This is a corker of a place, full of magical people, that puts all other moons in the shade. Enter the solar system through Space Gate 14 and see for yourself.

The Gargantuan Dictionary of Cosmic Crackers

The moon is a ball of delight that dances alongside Earth and isn't that far from the sun. It is home to loads of really cool moon people who like to live life to the full. Get to know them; they're great.

The Babbage Dictionary of Magical Moons

The moon is a big ball of fun held captive by the Earth's gravity. The people here are madder than a box of gizzpips. Worth a special journey.

The Omniverse Guide to Special Places

MOON PEOPLE – WHAT WE LOOK LIKE

You might be wondering what moon people look like. Well, we look great! Some of us look quite sensational, and some of us look amazing.

We are a bit like Earth people. We have a head, two arms and two legs, and we like chocolate. I suppose that's where our similarities end, though.

For a start, we have magnetic skin. This means that we don't really need pockets because we can stick keys and coins to our skin if we need to.

Having magnetic skin can be a problem in a restaurant, though, because most of the cutlery ends up all over us if we sit too close to the table.

Moon people have big heads. We call them think tanks. On average, a moon person's bonce measures 90cm in circumference and weighs about 6kg. That is about the same size and weight as a moon puffball – those funny little creatures you might see from time to time rolling down the side of craters shouting 'Weeeeeeeeeeeeeeeeeeeeeeeeeee'.

Moon people have such big noddles because they have three brains to accommodate. There are two large brains that wrap around a smaller brain, like a pair of hands holding a ball. The small brain or nugget is the brain we use when we are growing up, and it contains all our memories and experiences from birth to 10 years. It smells of blue cheese.

The two larger brains or nugget mitts protect the small brain and make sure nothing is forgotten or leaks out. If we want to remember anything from our first ten years of life, the nugget mitts gently squeeze the nugget to help release the information required. Squeezing too hard only results in moongook being uttered, which is completely unfathomable! When everyone reaches a shoe size of 74, the nugget mitts take over responsibility for all new learning and decision-making.

Our brains are well-protected by a triple cranium. The outer cranium is made of a material tougher than diamond called nogginz. The middle cranium is made of a very strong metal called filbert and the inner cranium is made of sage. Surrounding all three brains is yet another layer of protection; a special flexible membrane called acumen. This ultra-thin layer of brain slime prevents micro-organisms snooping around and causing trouble.

You will notice that all moon people have a little transparent square patch between their eyes that contains a bubble. This is a spirit level and shows how happy we are.

If the bubble sits perfectly in the middle, then that is a good sign that all is well and couldn't be better. If you can't see the bubble at all, then it's best to stay out the way.

Moon people don't have ears. We don't need them. We can still hear, though. Our hearing is so good we can hear a pin drop on Mars. The fact that there are no pins on Mars is beside the point.

Instead of ears, we have tiny receptors that pick up vibrations that are then channelled to our brains. These receptors are less than 1mm in size and travel the circumference of our heads in a continuous line.

They are skin-coloured too, and so cannot be seen. Not that we are vain. Our appearance is important to us, but we don't look in the mirror every five minutes like some Earth people do.

Speaking of which, if we want to see what we look like, then we use our hands. All we have to do is place the palm of our hands in front of us and we see our own reflection. Each hand palm is made of a special reflective skin, and so acts like a mirror.

Hands are especially useful for looking at the back of our heads after a haircut, a storm or if a bugnap decides to nest there. This explains why you will hardly see a mirror inside the toilets on the moon. We just use our hands.

There are mirrors on the moon, though, so there is no need to panic, but they work differently to Earth mirrors. When you look into a moon mirror, then your reflection is stretched sideways. We have made them this way because we think reflections can be a bit too serious sometimes.

Moon people have quite amazing hair. One popular style is Static Nut, a sort of sticky-up hairstyle that makes us look like we are in a state of constant shock.

To achieve this look, we wash our hair in a special statically charged shampoo. This makes our hair stand on end when it is dry and can last for about two days.

Try not to confuse the Static Nut style with people who actually look like this all of the time. That's the hair they were born with and it sticks up permanently, so try not to laugh.

Another popular style people go wild about is Peacock's Bum. This is when people add iridescent green, blue and purple feathers into their hair taken from moonpeas, which are a cloned version of Earth peacocks. They are fed on rainbow scorpions from Venus and kaleidoscope juice from the Jig Crater.

A lot of moon people like to grow their hair as tall as possible and then cut holes into it. This style is called The Cheesy Beehive, because it tends to look like Swiss cheese and is about the size of a beehive.

The Cheesy Beehive can make moon people look taller than they actually are which is why some moon people grow their hair this way. Moon people tend not to be that tall. The tallest moon person that has ever lived is Mini-moo Glogjog from Crater 99, measuring 28.92 hoobs, which is about 177cm tall.

One very popular style amongst moon teenagers is the Number Nut. This involves wearing lots of numbers in your hair, each one made out of the tightly interwoven strands of a moon donkey.

Some people wear a head full of numbers from 0-9, whereas other people like to wear just certain numbers like 1, 4 and 9. The numbers are normally coloured differently to each other, so they stand out.

Alpha Mops have caught on again recently in certain craters. These are letters of the moon alphabet and are worn in exactly the same way as Number Nuts, although they tend to be made from the hair of moon wibs.

All moon hair smells of popcorn, which is strange because most people wash their hair in tomato ketchup.

It's worth knowing that moon people have naturally curly hair. In the Northern Hemisphere of the moon this will curl in a clockwise direction and in the Southern Hemisphere it will grow in an anti-clockwise direction. If you are bald, then this point is irrelevant. By the way, bald men are considered very handsome on the moon.

Be careful to distinguish between moon men and moon women, as it is women who have facial hair. Men have no facial hair whatsoever. They do have a lot of foot hair, though. It is considered attractive for a woman to grow rainbow-coloured sideburns and grow her knee hair quite long.

Apart from awesome head hair, moon people have remarkable smiles and elastic mouths. Our smiles are at least twice the width of a human smile and they last five times as long.

Moon people love smiling, mostly because they have a lot to smile about living on the moon. Spend two weeks on the moon and you won't be able to stop smiling for at least a month when you get home.

At full stretch, our mouths can open up to about 30cm. Look inside and you'll find an impressive set of 75 teeth that glow in the dark and replace themselves once every year on our birthdays. Our teeth are also self-cleaning, so you won't find many toothbrushes on the moon.

Our tongues tend to be a talking point for Earth people because they change colour according to what we eat. If we eat anything acidic then our tongues turn a glittery blue and white colour. If we eat anything non-acidic then our tongues turn yellow. If we eat foods that are both acidic and non-acidic then our tongues turn grasshopper green.

Our noses tend to be long and thin, with six holes up and down their length on each side. These holes help us to breathe in different atmospheres and they are good at smelling danger, smelling a rat and smelling anything a bit fishy.

They are also excellent for sniffing out trouble. Our nasal range is so good, we can detect scents one million times more acutely than a bloodhound. That's not to be sniffed at, but it can be a pain. It means that we tend to pick up on all sorts of smells, and believe us when we say that there are more unpleasant smells than agreeable ones. Have you ever smelt a gack-tunker's armpit after an arm-wrestling match? It will knock you into next week.

Moon people have eyes at the front and back of their heads and we can see in the dark because we are blessed with infra-red vision. Face eyes are detachable, whereas those in the back of the head are there for good.

Back eyes are especially useful for walking backwards when the sun is dazzling your face eyes. The biggest problem moon people face having eyes in the back of their heads is hair. Most of the time we can't see what's behind us because our hair is in the way. Bald people don't have this problem, of course, which is why they have the best eyesight of anyone on the moon.

Some moon people have been born with an eye on top of their heads. This gives them a bird's eye view and is invaluable for spotting a bird dropping making a scene. They are great for keeping an eye on the weather, too.

One thing you will see a lot of on the moon is moon people crying their eyes out. These are normally tears of happiness and mostly happen after hearing a funny story or seeing someone fall over. Back eyes are useful for helping to locate the eyes that have fallen out. Once located, eyes can be picked up and placed back in their sockets again without a problem, although giving them a quick wash before doing so is advised, as grit, dust and muck can seriously impair vision.

Not all eyes are replaced though as some roll away and disappear from view. These are normally eaten by moon dogs or pecked at by moon crows. Moon people always carry spare eyeballs or just borrow an eyeball from someone else. This explains why you might see some moon people with only one face eye – they've probably lent it to a friend so they can get home.

All moon people are born with a mind's eye, but not everyone can see with it. Using your mind's eye takes years of practice and some people remain mind blind for their whole life. People that can see with their mind's eye have the ability to see inside the souls of other people and see the world as they see it. This is a rare gift, and only a few people can manage it.

Moon people's voices tend to be very high-pitched. This is because the atmosphere contains quite a bit of hinklepix. It also contains sodium and that makes our saliva very salty. What we are really good at doing is throwing our voices. You might think that someone is behind you when in fact they are nowhere near. This can be useful if you see your friend up ahead of you and you can't be bothered to walk over. You can basically have a conversation at a distance of about 500m by throwing voices to and fro without needing to shout at the top of your voice.

Voice throwing can throw a lot of Earth people when they first arrive on the moon. The voices are real, but the people that have thrown them can't always be seen. Some Earth people begin to believe they are going crazy. Most visitors get used to the voice-throwing antics of moon people, but some just can't cope and leave the moon with voices ringing in their ears.

Moon people tend to burp a lot. Our burps have been measured at 140 decibels, which is about the same noise level as the tummy-rumble of a Jeg-pester. We never really know when a burp is on its way. It just comes out. This always seems to happen mid-sentence, which can be annoying.

Burps stink quite a bit as well. If someone burps in your face whilst you are having a chat, then just take things in your stride and try not to breathe in too much. Making a fuss really isn't worth it.

The arms of moon people are about twice the size of our heads, and we can twizzle them around 360 degrees without them breaking. Our arms might not show much in the way of muscle, but we hold a lot of strength, so don't be fooled. Try having an arm wrestle with us or shaking our hands if you don't believe us.

Speaking of hands, we have six long fingers on each hand. Our fingers are magnetic, extendable up to 1m and have a torch at the end of each fingertip. These are ideal for picking noses, superb for picking magnetic moon strawberries, and just the job for searching in drains for lost coins and keys.

Moon people have quite extraordinary tummies that open up like cupboards for storing things in. These are lined with fur and tend to be excellent places for keeping newborn babies cosy and warm.

Men and women share the responsibility for looking after babies, which is why you will often see men with quite big bellies. Tummy pouches have their own oxygen supply so that babies can breathe.

Most moon people use their tummy pouches for carrying shopping and for keeping emergency items close by, such as a book, a slice of moon cheesecake or spare eyeballs. They are perfect for transporting bits and bobs, and this leaves our hands free to prod, poke, point, clap or generally swish about.

Did you know that moon people don't wee? That's because we don't have bladders. All wastewater is excreted through our skin and evaporates on contact with the air. This isn't as bad as it sounds. The fragrance might not be your cup of tea, but it's worth remembering that a pong to one person is a bouquet to someone else.

If you don't like someone's smell, then it is rude to walk away from them in the middle of a conversation. Leave at the beginning instead and make it clear why you are on your way.

Moon people are blessed with having swivel hips. These can twist 270 degrees, a bit like an owl can turn its head. This proves invaluable in a running race, as you can pull faces at your competitors and try to put them off. Swivel hips are also useful for standing in a queue when you get bored, and especially useful for dancing at parties. Moon people are excellent dancers.

Our legs have three joints, which make us pretty good at running, hopping, skipping and jumping. They tend to be quite bendy, and we can wrap them around our necks with little or no problem. We are natural yogis. This makes our lives a whole lot easier when there isn't much legroom between seats. We have two pairs of knees, and they all sweat honey. We call them the Bee's Knees.

It's worth warning you in advance that our feet stink. It's something we are proud of. In between our toes, we like to grow little balls of cheese, and this gives our feet their distinctive odour. The cheese is edible and tastes very cheesy. It can be eaten as a snack or enjoyed before a main course, but most moon people collect the balls and melt them into a liquid for drinking. It is considered good manners to offer someone a glass of your foot cheese when they first step into your home.

The soles of our feet have natural grip and are made from a very fine and flexible type of material called Hoov-X. Of course, we do wear shoes, but many moon people like to paint their feet and design their own shoe styles. This is why you will see a lot of paint footprints everywhere.

Moon people are always stubbing their toes, so it's a good job they are made of steel. We are born with 13 toes – six on the left foot and seven on the right. People think this is related to the 13 black moons that orbit the moon, but no one really knows.

When it comes to clothes, moon people are real trendsetters. At one time, it was fashionable for moon people in the Northern Hemisphere to wear copper and fibreglass, whilst those in the Southern Hemisphere wore spun bronze, but this soon died out after the craze for wearing cork and bamboo.

You will probably see many young moon people wearing clothes made from recycled materials, such as cans, bottle tops, cardboard, paper, glass beads and plastic bags.

Teenagers mostly wear clothes that show moving images called Vision Fits. These amazing clothes are made up of hundreds of flexible panels that show fantasy flashback and flashforward dream sequences. This makes a lot of people stare at teenagers, which is precisely what they want you to do.

Teenagers also like wearing Swaps. These are clothes that can change colour simply by pressing a button. The more buttons there are on a garment, the more colours you have to choose from. Although young people like to think they are fashion icons, it's worth remembering that the best-dressed things on the moon are salads.

Older people tend to wear Canny Clothes – intelligent digital clothing that monitors the body and conducts health scans throughout the day. These smart clothes check heart function, breathing, temperature, skin condition, and blood circulation. They are solar-powered and come in all colours except Martian Red and Paradise Green. These thinking clothes are also self-cleaning and never require washing or ironing.

Moon people are very patient people, and nothing gets on our nerves. Well, not much, anyway. We tend to see red and get frustrated by people who think in black and white, and by anyone who can't see the wood for the trees.

We also get irritated by anyone who can't see beyond the end of their nose, and people that blow hot and cold. Other things that drive us nuts are people who don't store their elastic bands in the refrigerator, people who like licking sellotape and people who talk to pavements. Actually, moon people get annoyed quite a lot.

We can't believe that some Earth people don't think we even exist. Well, we are very much alive and kicking, although kicking isn't something we do a great deal of. We prefer to hop.

CHILDREN

Moon children normally begin their lives as one of four squidgets. Quads are the norm on the moon, whereas one baby is considered highly unusual and normally makes the news.

Squidgets grow inside their mummies' tummies, which are all fluffy and cosy. They look like paper clips to start with, and then quickly develop into plump, squashy beans.

Squidgets are born after just four months, and for the first few weeks of their lives, they spend most of their day playing jigsaws and vomiting extremely sour honey. This has a surprisingly pleasant taste and it is used for cooking or catching moon flies. Jigsaw pieces covered in honey are delicious when fried and dipped in mayo-moonaise.

Squidgets also spend a lot of their day belching, which can be very noisy and rather smelly. A squidget belch can blow a candle out from 20 yards, and its aroma is enough to floor a moon dog for half an hour. As they get older, squidgets learn to recognise the power they have at their disposal, and execute as much mayhem as they can whilst retaining their cute factor. They can often be seen pointing their behinds into people's letterboxes; then running off.

You've probably worked out that squidgets can't really be trusted, but we still love them. They are incredibly naughty, but most of what they do is hilarious. We just have to pretend that we are not amused, even though we are. It's best not to let a squidget catch you laughing, though, because they can take it the wrong way. If they do see you giggling, then don't be surprised to find things stuffed into your shoes overnight and traps being left around the house for at least a week as revenge.

Squidgets get up to all sorts of things as they are growing up. They have been known to steal waterfalls, chase intelligent gases, cover moon castles in jam, scare their own reflections, and burp inside other people's memories. They also like spreading nettle rash on yellow numbers, blackmailing spiders, pretending to be camels, brainwashing frogs until they are dizzy, juggling yunks until they are sick, standing on one finger in puddles and catapulting ideas into orbit.

Some of this behaviour might surprise you, but you will soon realise that moon people can do things that you can't. You might call them special powers, but we just see them as a normal part of who we are. It's what we are born with.

You might think moving objects using mind over matter or 'mind touch' is amazing, whereas we find it weird that you can't move things using mind power. Squidgets are born with this ability, and love to roll pencils, turn the pages of a book, bend spoons or play the accordion in mid-air. They find their mind-bending skills funny to start off with, but they soon learn how useful they are and seldom abuse them.

Mind over matter has many practical uses. For example, you might be carrying a tray of food from the kitchen to another room and need to open the door. You could put your tray on the floor, but why bother, when you can use your mind to open the door instead?

One thing squidgets are very good at doing is sending their thoughts to another squidget without speaking.

This is called telepathy. You lose the power to do this after the age of ten, which is why all moon adults, except teachers, are hopeless at it. Teachers spend 10 years training how to do it again.

Visit a school and arrange to observe a class for yourself. What you will see is a teacher standing at the front of the class in total silence. You'll notice that none of the squidgets are talking, either. Yet there is a really lively lesson going on. The teacher is asking loads of questions and the squidgets are deep in discussion with each other, sharing their ideas. To you, nothing is going on, but in reality, there is a heap of learning taking place.

Telepathic teaching is the way we have always done it, but Earth visitors are left speechless when they see it for the first time. Isn't that ironic? Anyway, moon schools are very calm and quiet places. This explains why children learn so much there.

When the school day is over, squidgets speak out loud so we know what they have been doing. You may have trouble understanding them, but we are tuned into their developing language

Squidgets talk so fast they tend to wix up their murds, which can be confusing, but it's serfectly pimple once you get the hang of it! They tend to flip them like pancakes, and do it without really realising. Don't be surprised if you hear one saying they don't like eating parrots and keys. We consider word flipping in this context really mad banners.

Children's names are popular on the moon, which might sound odd, but not everyone has a first name here. Everyone has a surname, though, and this is always after the place where you were born. If this was Library 16 in Moon Corridor 4 of the Crink Crater, then your last name would be Library 16. Obviously, it is better to be born in some places than others. No one really wants their last name to be Hard Shoulder, Emergency Exit or Mountain Toilet. The top ten boys and girls' first names for the last decade are as follows:

Boys – first names	Girls – first names
1. Bronk	1. Dimp
2. H2-Go	2. Nuz
3. Quiznest	3. Jigpipple
4. Pockerpan	4. Falala-lalaFa
5. Gasplank	5. Fixfaxfootfix
6. Fn20Fn	6. Noddles
7. Redshift	7. Dishdoodle
8. Windjig	8. PoloX
9. Zo-Zo	9. Mashquacker
10. J	10. Pinkle

Moon children are allowed to change their first names when they get to about 12, but only by swapping the letters around in their existing name. This isn't much fun if your name only has one letter, but quite a treat if it's Crizzynitpat-pootybun. When you are an adult moon person, then you can change your name once a week if you want to, and many people do, although friends find this frustrating.

Earth tourists sometimes give birth on the moon, which is truly a fantastic moment but parents can get carried away sometimes and opt for a moon name for their child. This seldom works, because moon names and Earth names just don't mix or sound right together. I mean, Gasplank Jones, Dishdoodle Smith and Mashquacker McDonald? You Earth people can be a bit over the top sometimes.

There are various meaningful milestones in a squidget's life. They move through seven stages of growth. Below, you will see just a few of the things they can do at each point of development. See how they differ from the development of your children.

By the end of Phase 1, moon children can:

- Flip a flop
- Cut a light rod into eight pieces
- Engrave a feeling into ice
- Chase an impression back into its reflection
- Mouthwash with adjectives
- Tie shoelaces with one hand
- Ride a Monoflipper without magnetisers
- Sidestep the ugly truth

By the end of Phase 2, moon children can:

- Clink a clunk
- Complete a 1,000 piece jigsaw blindfolded
- Sing the moon anthem forwards and backwards
- Dissolve an atrocious spelling
- Draw a horse, ride a horse and talk to a horse
- Negotiate the safe release of a pigeon held captive by a Nag-Nadger
- Accurately measure 50g of sunshine

- Sandwich two numbers
- Save a pretty penny from being trodden on

By the end of Phase 3, moon children can:

- Pizzle a fuzzle
- Poach a boo-boo egg without cracking it
- Levitate sideways for at least 2m
- Insulate a feeling and protect it from predators
- Escape from a nightmare
- Smell sounds and hear smells
- Dental floss a shimp dangle
- Recycle opportunities
- Corner a word
- Spotlight a future

By the end of Phase 4, moon children can:

- Dingle a fingle
- Dissect a shadow
- Bake an idea without burning it
- Drive a moon dish independently
- Play chess with Siamese moon gerbils
- Colonise a cranky computer program
- Outfox a stopwatch
- Disorientate a soundtrack
- Design a daft octopus with spiral eyes
- Excavate a dribble of brown fabric sick
- Unjumble a Frumble's mumble

By the end of Phase 5, moon children can:

- Squiggle a niggle

- Mesmerise a poisonous moon toad
- Hear the conversations of a moon minxie's fingerprints
- Rotate ideas 360 degrees
- Make a chocolate soufflé
- Evaporate puddles
- Weigh a kaleidoscope reflection
- Climb into a cartoon without getting hurt
- Control a chilli pepper remotely
- Reconstruct a space chimp
- Translate a kite's hard feelings
- Babysit a naughty xylophone

By the end of Phase 6, moon children can:

- Shimp a shump
- Smell gravity
- Sculpt their own daydreams
- Calm down a distressed moon cube
- Teach a scarecrow to tap dance
- Stack 20 ping-pong balls without glue
- Taste soundwaves
- Cross-stitch silver linings using cloud 9 thread
- Photograph a shout
- Scatter a giggawhizz
- Gurgle a pot of bish
- Wrestle time
- Balance a pencil on a blade of air
- Skim an idea across a thought lake
- Intercept a shard of broken silence
- Sweep away fears without inhaling the dust
- Chill a radio wave

By the end of Phase 7, moon children can:

- Tinkle a tonkle
- Dissect wishes
- Rehabilitate naughty moon clowns
- Peep inside other people's souls
- Shrink-wrap a phobia
- Read clouds
- Commute between brainstorms
- Isolate a spark and freeze it in a cube sphere
- Reverse an unwanted dream into a tight space without using a mirror
- Divide a creative thought into quarters
- Measure a complaint to within 1mm
- Pirouette at the heart of happiness
- Melt a dream without leaving any lumps
- Spiritually nourish an angry attitude

It's worth remembering that these stages are only a guide, and represents a fraction of what moon children can do. Some moon children have been known to perform the skills of Phase 5 children by the end of Phase 1.

It can be a worrying time for parents. Some parents fret if, by the end of Phase 4, their children aren't aquadextrous, can't talk with buzz birds or bog-snorkel with cuboids, but this happens in time, so it's best to focus on what they can do, rather than what they can't. It's actually quite common for quads to develop at completely different rates to each other, so comparing them is pretty pointless.

Moon children have a very calming effect on Earth children, which is why the moon is a popular place for

Earth families to visit. Earth children who are notorious for being like headless hurricanes with a migraine get lots of cuddles from moon children and soon learn to calm down.

They do things they would never do on Earth, like paint messages in the sky, cook anagrams, hunt moon flowers, play basketball with ghost cats, explore sky villages, read moonflake X-rays, spy on brain snails, whistle through the nose, pillow fight moon troopers, eat parrot cheese, wrestle wigs, hypnotise clouds and sail on sound waves.

By the time Earth children leave the moon, they are all fluffy and blissful.

Moon children smell a lot. We don't mean they whiff, although many do – we mean they sniff the air around them. This is the main way they learn a language and build their vocabulary. You see, when words are spoken, they enter the atmosphere and generally linger there for about 30 seconds before gravity drags them to the ground. You can't see them, but you can smell them. So before the words hit the ground, moon children sniff them up and their brains absorb them and file them.

When there is a lot of chatter between adults, you will see children sniffing around them and it might look like they are full of a cold. Words that are rejected by the brain are sneezed out. Rejected words include any swear word or any word that is misspelt.

When a word is sneezed out, it is blown into pieces, so that its individual letters are scattered here, there and everywhere and have no chance of finding each other again. This is particularly important if the word is a swear word, because it has no chance of reforming.

Misspelt words are considered almost as hazardous, and so they are left to fend for themselves. If children sneeze a lot around adults, then you will know that the language adults are using involves a lot of swearing or they are bad spellers.

All words and letters that end up on the ground are eaten by microbes called boff-gigs. Look at a boff-gig under a microscope and you will see it is just one big alphabet soup of nonsense. They are about the size of a full stop.

If you see moon children with runny noses, then you'll know that they are ready for a sleep. A stream of honeyed snotgoo is always a sign of tiredness and should not be ignored, as it stains clothes orange. The snotgoo glows in the dark and dries up when a moon child has had enough rest.

Moon children love to play. They normally play inside each other's dreams, where they are safe and we know where to find them.

They like to chase sandwiches, climb on the walls of space, parachute with pogo sticks, surf silly sentences, wiggle with wavelengths, tip toe around time zones, interview moon spiders, hug cuddles, bug snorkel with moon fizzers, swim under icequakes, shout at whispers, and play hide and seek with curiosity.

They also like to catch flies that taste of garlic bread. We wish they wouldn't, because they eat them and then always have rumbly tummies as a result.

A favourite game of moon children is to explore the inside of thought bubbles. To do this, they have to first catch one, which is easier than you think. Thought bubbles don't normally pop on contact with anything, so you can handle one without worry. You could even play mind tennis with one. They only pop when an idea inside becomes so big that it has nowhere else to go. If you are playing tennis at the time that a great idea makes an appearance, then it is possible a thought bubble could explode in the middle of a game.

To catch a thought bubble, you just have to be in the right place at the right time. Some are bigger than others, so this isn't normally an issue, as they can be spotted from a mile away. To get inside a captured thought bubble, moon children cover one part of it with hagmush mucus, and then make a hole in the bubble with a big stick and climb in. The mucus stops the bubble from bursting, as it is so sticky. Don't worry – this doesn't hurt the bubble, as they feel no pain.

Once inside thought bubbles, moon children like to swing on ideas, play seesaw with arguments, slide down dreams and speed skate with visions. To get out of a thought bubble, children tickle the inside with an illusion and the bubble froths, foams and then gently pops, so no one gets hurt. If you've never seen a thought bubble before, then you can see a collection in the think tank ideas aquarium in Crater 9.9, although none of the bubbles there are for catching.

Moon children do things that irritate adults sometimes. One annoying habit they have is trapping nightmares and then releasing them into wishing wells. This isn't popular because all wishes come true on the moon, and the sorts of wishes nightmares usually have aren't very pleasant. They normally involve something smelly.

Moon children like to blow kisses. This might sound harmless and you might even think that's a lovely thing to do, but when you blow a kiss on the moon, it's always a really wet one and they are full of slobber, which isn't easy to remove. They tend to miss their target, too, which means that many kisses blown end up going off course and landing on someone or something else. This typically leads to a lot of apologies being made and everyone getting embarrassed.

Moon children are good at drawing. They remember everything they see in minute detail and their drawings are on the awesome side of stunning. You might be wondering why this annoys us. Well, they use special talking pencils that describe the things they are drawing as they are being drawn. They are brutally honest when it comes to describing people, and they are quite frankly rude. Children know this, so they always draw pictures of their teachers and other adults they want to annoy.

Don't enter a staring competition with a moon child, because they can capture any secrets you may have by reading your mind. Some people don't mind because their secrets are old ones or past their sell-by date. These are called bottom secrets and don't tend to be that important, as they are normally common knowledge. Some people do mind, though, as their secrets are highly confidential and normally contain something highly embarrassing.

If a moon child manages to capture a top secret, then they quickly become bottom secrets, and things can get messy.

If moon children can't find an adult to play their staring tricks with, then they normally target a moon cat. As far as we know, moon cats have just as many secrets as the rest of us, and they try to avoid moon children as much as possible.

One creature that doesn't mind sharing secrets is the moon piff. These jet-black fuzzballs have eyes twice as big as their bellies. They are about the size of a chinchilla and three times as sweet. They spend a lot of their time eavesdropping, which means they pick up a lot of secrets in the course of a day.

Moon piff droppings are full of eaves. These are like little Chinese fortune cookies, and if you break one open, you will find a random secret inside belonging to someone. Names and addresses are not normally included. Moon children and moon piffs tend to get on rather well.

Despite their impishness and spells of mischief, moon children are delightful to be around and they fill our lives with unpredictable excitement. Their extreme strengths make them the most intelligent beings on the moon, and we respect them for that.

ANIMALS

There are some remarkable creatures found on and above the moon, as you might expect. As you crater-hop across the moon, you are bound to see moonpuffs. These little balls of fluff love rolling down the side of craters and can be great fun to watch. They are harmless and armless, and survive by licking the salt off crater stones. They also love the taste of echoes.

Moonpuff saliva helps to stop anyone from bleeding after a cut, as it glues broken skin together. Moonpuffs used to be hunted for their beautiful voices, but they are now protected by Solar Law 5629, which states,

'All moonpuffs have the right to sing their heads off and their hearts out and no one should lay a finger on them, otherwise there will be trouble.'

Oaf fish are animals you are bound to bump into when you are on the moon. If you don't, then they are bound to bump into you, because they are walking disasters. They aren't even proper fish.

Oaf fish come in two sizes: clumsy and very clumsy. These apologetic little creatures are always falling over their ridiculously oversized feet, and can't help but get themselves into a mess. Imagine a pair of clown's feet attached to two short hairy legs and the body of a hairy football with a smile. That's an oaf fish. They don't really have heads, because their eyes are part of their knees and they have eight buttered fingers and two thumbs on each hapless hand.

Oaf fish don't mean any harm, but they are accidents waiting to happen, which is why most moon people will avoid them wherever possible. If there is something to knock over, trip over, drop or break, then an oaf fish will find it. Oaf fish are desperate to be your friends, and although you might feel sympathetic towards them, our advice is to look busy and do something else!

In the fields of Zones 20-22 of the Northern Tip-Tops, you will see herds of windy wuffalubs. These unkempt creatures look as if the wind is blowing in their scrunched-up faces and their hair is constantly swept back. This is strange, because Zones 20-22 are completely windless.

Windy wuffalubs are about the same height as mangle horses from Neptune, but twice the width, which makes them great for hiding behind. Windy wuffalubs will spend most of their time reading, drinking parsnip juice or looking worried. They can be quite nosy and they are scared of the dark. At night, they change colour from a reddish-brown to white and their hooves sparkle. This helps them feel safe.

When windy wuffalubs are born, they run away from their mothers straight away. This is dangerous, because it's not unusual for a mother to see her newborn as prey by mistake.

If you take a trip across the Southern Hemisphere, then you will see thousands of creatures dotting the landscape that look like wheelbarrows. These are shubdungs. They have two handles sticking out of a large shell and a wheel at the front. Some people call them turtle-barrows. Rather than carrying loads around, they just carry themselves. Well, they try to.

Shubdungs mostly rely on the wind to move them from place to place or kind people that happen to be passing. Some shubdungs stay in one place for months and months without ever moving. This doesn't bother them that much, because they like to take things easy and their shells contain plenty of stories, which they feed off. They are also very friendly, which is why people don't mind pushing them when out for a walk. In fact, shubdungs make great company because they always have a tale to tell, and they love sharing them with anyone that will listen.

Moon walkers will push shubdungs when on a ramble and learn all sorts of interesting things along the way, some of it useful. Many people push a shubdung for a little way, have a rest and then carry on pushing when they have got their breath back, as they can be heavy.

When you have finished pushing a shubdung, it is polite to leave them in a sensible place and let them know you are on your way. Remember, they can't see you and so if you just leave without saying goodbye they will just carry on offloading stories thinking that you are still there.

The moon atlas turtles of the Southern Hemisphere have a map of the Northern Hemisphere and all their craters printed on the outside of their shells. The moon atlas turtles of the Northern Hemisphere have a map of the Southern Hemisphere on theirs. This isn't that helpful. We don't know why they don't just swap places with each other, because if you are lost in the Southern Hemisphere, then a map of the Northern Hemisphere isn't much use. Moon scientists have tried relocating the turtles, but after a day they walk back home again.

Scientists have since found out that moon atlas turtles from the south react badly to the gravity in the north. The main side effect of their relocation was that they produced winged beetles when they urinated. They also found they couldn't whistle.

Moon atlas turtles from the north didn't settle in the south because they found the shadows were too noisy, the microwaves weren't as friendly, and the echoes ignored them. Moon atlas turtles in the north and south breathe in unison and fall asleep at exactly the same time.

Watch out for hedgehog rhinos. These creatures aren't to be messed with. They are full of anger and they steam for most of the day, getting worked up about something, normally something trivial. They have blood that boils, they foam at the mouth and they regularly get their knickers in a twist.

A hedgehog rhino is an obnoxious beast covered in spikes with a head full of short fuses. No one knows why hedgehog rhinos are so cheesed off, but we think it might be something to do with their pink hooves.

Hedgehog rhinos don't tend to pick fights with other creatures, but they will fight each other. They are born with magnetic heads and bottoms. This means that when a rhino with a north head charges a rhino with a south head, they attract each other and they spend ages trying to pull themselves apart. This is hilarious to watch. What is even more comical is seeing one rhino attempting to walk away from a duel. You work it out, but remember, opposites attract.

Things that give hedgehog rhinos the goat include the price of slug lumps, imitation eyebrows, poetic odours, curtains, idea boxes, space scratches, and indecisive pomegranates. They also have no patience for uprooted myths, empty tents, late night stories, bitter lemons and polka dot dreams. They love eating knisper birds.

One creature stands head and shoulders above the rest and they are tunks. These remarkable birds can glide for 16 days without beating their wings and can sleep in mid-air while gliding at 75mph. They do this backwards and upside down. Some forget to fly high enough, which is why over 10,000 tunks a year die from smashing into moonscrapers.

Tunks actually suffer from vertigo and are quite often airsick. A tunk's hexagonal eye is larger than its brain, but that doesn't mean it's clueless. A tunk eye is so clever that it can position itself anywhere on a head to get the best view.

A tunk's brain is so full of brain cells they sometimes leak out and fall to Earth as raindrops. If they land on your head, then they run into your ears and find a nice place to sit in your brain, where there is normally plenty of room. This may be a blessing or a curse, depending on the brain cell. Some contain really useful information like how to fix a moon sky-bike that has run out of pep, and some are completely useless, such as how much wind a cow on Neptune releases in an hour. Tunks don't worry about losing brain cells, because they can regenerate them.

Tunks live in communal nests of about 500, and they are a work of art. They use their sharp beaks to pierce holes along the edge of small moon clouds. They then make a nest by stitching clouds together with rainbows. The nests hover 100m above the ground, out of harm's way – not that anyone wants to harm these wonderful constructions.

Even if the nests were threatened in any way, the tunks would soon know about it, because of their acute sense of hearing. They can hear a pin drop on Earth or a tiptum cry in the solar system above our own. A tiptum is a sort of mouse, by the way: an ecstatic little creature with three pink ears, fluffy orange shoulder-length hair and toes made of krypton. It only cries out of happiness. Even if anything was silly enough to try and get near a tunk homestead, tunks can make themselves invisible and move location without worry.

Another creature that will grab your attention is a fliffy-flaff. You might see them in the street eating fluff if you are in the right place at the right time. They are about the size of a Martian hen, and they walk backwards, spitting feathers. They can blink 100 times a second, which is obviously so fast that no one can really see this happening. This makes us wonder who actually knows whether this is true or not.

One thing is certain, though, and that is that a fliffy-flaff can see with its eyes closed. Its tongue can reach right inside its skull. It does this so it can clean the inside, where bits of moon dust can gather and where old crusty ideas get stuck between old nightmares and interrupted daydreams. A fliffy-flaff can sing four tunes at once. Individually, these tunes are sublime, but together, they sound like bagpipes fighting with haggis armed with jazz.

Fortunately, fliffy-flaffs don't like singing on their own that much. When the whole nest sings, the sound is majestic. This makes moon people float horizontally 1m above the ground and their teeth change colour from sapphire to bottle green. If Earth tourists hear a fliffy-flaff choir, their toes tingle and they start to dance.

You are bound to see moon cats wherever you are on the moon. Moon cats have no tails or whiskers, but they do have three hearts. This means they live for over 1,000 years. They are pretty laid-back creatures, but occasionally they suffer from stress. If they worry about worrying too much, then they end up curling into a ball. They do this until they get hungry.

Moon cats have a diet you might find pretty disgusting, but they'd probably find your diet hard to stomach or understand. They have three stomachs, which each digest their favourite foods. They like eating the toenails of nipnaps (winged, pig-like creatures that fly at low altitude), clookplops (a sort of moon mango that shoot up from 2,000-year-old craters), and mishslaps (luminous purple stalactites of cheese).

Moon cats will also eat the remains of anything struck by lightning, as this can be a rich source of energy. If moon cats eat too much, they fill up with gas and float up into space, where they point their rear to the southern end of the universe and press release. Not surprisingly, moon cats are related to crackle-natters and slingpests.

When moon dogs see moon cats, they start to chase them, which is, of course, a hopeless exercise, because moon cats can camouflage themselves. Moon dogs are also pretty daft and have quite poor eyesight. They are also rubbish at running.

Don't be afraid of moon dogs when you see them. These very ugly creatures can look intimidating, but they mean no harm. They have two sets of teeth: one set in their mouth and another set in their throats. These look very sharp, but they are actually very soft, which is why you can feed them without worrying about your fingers.

Moon dogs have four noses and they love sniffing around, mostly around each other. They also have 12 flat brains, but only use one of them. This is a huge shame and a massive loss to the universe, because they have the potential to be amazing.

Their brains look like buttons, and they all have five holes. They are attached together with pieces of brain thread, which run through the centre holes of each button. The pieces of thread are connected to their spine, and they send e-mails to the body about what to do and how to act. These messages often get sent to the wrong part of the body, or they get confused. This explains why moon dogs don't wag their tails, but their tails wag them.

Moon dogs love running upside down across ceilings. This drives everyone mad, because they leave their paw prints everywhere, and they aren't easy to remove.

Moon dogs are hardly inconspicuous. They are about 2m from nose to tail, hairy on one side and bald on the other side, which is covered in tattoos of eyeballs. Moon dogs also glow in the dark, and so does their urine. This is actually quite handy, because it lights up poorly-lit moon tracks at night.

Moon dogs have quite an annoying habit of vomiting in public. They do this after they have eaten too many moon pigeons, ulalalas (long, crinkly poles with the same taste as Earth bananas), packets of glue, or capital letters.

They love capital letters, and will lick them off moon signs everywhere. This is why you might see a sign saying 'Welcome to the oon.' When they are sick, they not only bring up the contents of their stomach, but also the stomach itself. The stomach hangs from a moon dog's mouth for a moment before being swallowed back again.

Moon dogs do have a number of other disgusting habits, though, which is why they can be so unpopular with many people as a choice of pet. For example, they squirt excrement on their legs because they think it looks fashionable, and they burp clouds of yellow gas because they think it's funny. It isn't.

Moon dogs bark, but they do so ultrasonically, which means that we cannot hear them, so it doesn't bother us. It just looks strange to see a dog putting heart and soul into a bark without the sound effects.

One thing we can hear, though, is their snoring. When a moon dog snores, it is like an orchestra of pneumatic drills. This is another reason why moon people don't really like them as pets. They are quite simply the most ineffective guard dogs in the whole solar system.

Try not to let a moon dog lick you, because you will get covered in a warm mottled blue slime that is similar in power to permanent ink and takes ages to wash off. This explains why some moon people you meet have blue smears over their faces.

Moon dogs are hyperactive creatures and seldom rest. In fact, they are on the go nearly all day. The only time they stand still is when they see a squiff-quacker. These are transparent snakes that appear from behind curtains in the sky.

Only moon dogs can see transparent objects, which is just as well really, because the idea of seeing snakes in the sky would put you off your tea. They see things we can't, and so when they seem to be barking at nothing, they are definitely barking at something. On the moon, nothing is always something, even when it doesn't appear to be anything.

If you visit the far, far side of the moon, and head for the DK8 crater, then chances are you will find mobbles getting under your feet. These fluffy and very likeable creatures are a bit like slippers, but with lots of mad hair covering their eyes. Actually, they are slippers. You see, you can actually slip your feet into a pair of mobbles, and they'll take you places you've never been, as well as places you don't want to go to. Don't worry about hurting them when you step into a pair, as they are tough little cookies.

Be careful, though – they might all look the same, but they aren't. To the untrained eye, mobbles look identical, but lift their fur and you'll see that their eyes are very different.

There are three types of mobbles. Some have copper eyes; some have glass eyes, and the rarest have glazed eyes. It's just a piece of advice, but if you do slip into a pair of mobbles, then just check that they are a pair, because you could end up wearing a copper-eyed mobble on one foot and a glass-eyed mobble on the other. This will only end in tears.

It's always better to go for a true pair – that way, you won't be in the middle of an argument. One mobble wants to turn right and the other wants to turn left, leaving you doing the splits whilst everyone else is in stitches. You are probably thinking that if this happens, you could just slip the mobbles off your feet. If only. Once they are on, they are on. They tend to grip your feet, and the only way to get them off is by negotiating, which normally involves some sort of payment.

Each crater on the moon tends to house different species, and a visit to the Nirage Crater (100 miles from the Crater of Lights) is a must. You will find three main animals here: faffers, bagwafts and blonks.

These amazing creatures are all very similar in size to an Earth sheep, but instead of being covered in wool, they grow edible shoelaces as a body covering. They taste remarkably good and they don't mind if you pick one or two from their backs if you are feeling peckish. Try not to take one from their belly, as this tends to hurt them when plucked.

Bagwafts tend to eat their own shoelaces, which some people find disgusting. They smell of snail crumble and pine cones and always have springtime in their eyes.

Faffers, bagwafts and blonks all belong to the same family of spit-pops – grazing animals that feed on the plentiful supply of iron filings found in the Nirage Crater. Their droppings make excellent magnets, and can be bought in gift shops across the crater.

All three animals are allowed to graze together, and they can be easily distinguished by the direction they adopt when feeding. Faffers all face east; bagwafts face west and blonks face south. Occasionally, you might get a faffer that faces west, but these tend to be the young. Bagwafts have been known to face north-northeast in the rain.

There are some important differences between faffers, bagwafts and blonks and the table below will help you distinguish between them.

	Faffers	Bagwafts	Blonks
Sneeze speed	300 mph	175 mph	425 mph
Distance travelled by voice	4.5km	15km	22km
Backward flips per min	3	6	9
Time spent giggling per day	5 hrs 25 mins	2 hrs 35 mins	15 mins
Length of nightmares	125cm	85cm	205cm
Iron filings eaten per day	13,089	8,711	606
Number of jokes per day	5	120	32
0-60 mph	20 secs	14 mins	N/A max speed 43mph
Length of nose hair	20cm	12cm	56cm
Amount of honey drunk in 1 week	8 jars	33 jars	0 – allergic to honey

One thing you will notice staying on the moon is the amount of flags we have here. You are bound to see fields and fields of flags being planted by niff-wicks, which are creatures that look a bit like Earth meerkats. These triangular flags are mostly blue, yellow, green and red and they stand about 30cm from the ground. From a distance, they look like a carpet of flowers. The thing is, we don't know why niff-wicks plant these flags, and we don't know where they get them from.

In some parts of the moon, we had to remove the flags, because they had taken over the land a bit. This wasn't popular with niff-wicks, and they simply planted more. We leave niff-wicks to it now, because they aren't causing us any harm and they do make the moon look very colourful. We know very little about niff-wicks, but we do know that they store eggs in their mouths, they smell of lavender and their bones are made of blue crystals.

So those are a few of the animals that live on the moon. If you get time, perhaps you could research some of the other creatures you will find here. We recommend reading about gumwidges, bricklebiffers, gasbags, and starry-eyed clugnuts to start with, before moving onto the brainboxed dartfips of Crater Nu and the jick nibblers of Crater Crox 2.

PLANTS

There are plants galore on the moon. They can be divided into two types: intelligent plants and daft plants. Both types can speak, but one speaks when spoken to, whilst the other just jabbers on and will just get on your nerves.

The main difference between an intelligent plant and a daft plant is that an intelligent plant will move habitat if the mineral supply is poor, the climate takes a turn for the worse or the water supply dries up. Clever plants waste no time looking for somewhere new to live if the going gets a bit rough. They simply up roots and find a new patch to settle down in. Daft plants frequently die mid-sentence because they don't plan ahead.

Try not to get into a conversation with a daft plant if you can help it. They tend to talk non-stop gibberish, pretend to know everything about everything and they don't have a good word to say about intelligent plants.

They will try to convince you that growing and eating certain types of food are bad for your health or have unpleasant side effects.

If a daft plant says that you should avoid eating figglenibs because they give you bad wind then take it with a pinch of salt. Figglenibs are particularly good for seeing in the park and they are full of vitamins. Parks are notoriously difficult to see in, because they are always busy places. Figglenibs help you to see what's going on because they slow down your eyeballs and stop them moving so fast. This gives your eyes a chance to focus and see more of what is going on.

Daft plants are not really to be trusted, although moon children like them because they tell lots of lies. Gilding the lily and leading people up the garden path are things that daft plants do best.

Amazingly, some people keep daft plants as houseplants because they are entertaining, provide a bit of company and are excellent smoke detectors. Most people don't have them as houseplants, though, because they are rude to guests, they never stop moaning and they smell of stale sweat when left alone.

One daft plant to beware of is the shrinking moon violet. This arrogant flower named itself to dupe you into thinking it's a walkover, but it couldn't be further from the truth.

The shrinking moon violet is a shockingly ill-mannered gutsy plant that doesn't beat around the bush. It's a fiend! Try answering it back on any subject and you'll find yourself on the receiving end of a barrage of abuse.

Shrinking moon violets should not be given to anyone on Valentine's Day because they tend to speak their minds and find faults as a hobby. It will come as no surprise to find out that shrinking moon violets are related to artificial flowers and fool no one. We tolerate this mad flower because its pollen is known to cure asthma and eczema in sufferers.

There are over 10,000 intelligent plants on the moon and they are all edible. Poisonous plants are non-existent, although some people say daft plants are full of toxic rudeness, which poisons the minds of others. Annoying as they are, daft plants can't kill you.

Intelligent plants are good for you because they are packed full of clever chemicals, calculating calories, and smart nutrients. Ask a plant what it can do for you and it will tell you.

Many people eat a plant whilst the plant is actually still talking. A plant might be in the middle of a sentence and never get to finish it because it is eaten alive.

Eating plants whilst they are talking might sound cruel, but they are better for you because they are fresher. You can literally hear words being chewed to pieces when you munch into one. If you have never witnessed this before, it might put you off, but trust us when we say that the plant feels no pain. The plant sees it as an honour to be eaten alive, as it knows it will be put to good use.

Intelligent plants or 'smarty plants', as some moon people call them, are very well educated. They are capable of speaking Latin and know every plant name under the sun by heart. Test one and find out.

Smarty plants know all their times tables, they can read camouflaged books, they appreciate art, play several instruments and they can recite poetry. They also have solar-powered dreams and they can outwit Mohican caterpillars. Smarty plants know a lot about cooking and will be able to tell you the best ways to prepare a dish.

Plants can see, hear and smell just like us, and love listening to music. They are also extremely ticklish and they enjoy a good joke. Intelligent plants are particularly good at doing crosswords in the rain and solving riddles in a drought and they also like drawing in the night.

Intelligent plants have a sixth sense and will be able to tell if you are telling the truth, so always play a straight bat. They know if you like them or not, and they instinctively know whether you are a secret agent for daft plants.

Unfortunately, this happens. Some moon people work on behalf of daft plants and will try to extract juices and important information about growing. Daft plants use this inside information to try and pass themselves off as intelligent plants.

Some say that this proves that daft plants aren't as daft as they look, but others disagree and say it proves that they are deceitful. Although intelligent plants are well known for their brains, the amount of magnetism in the soil can affect their judgement. It is thought that gravity hot spots with high concentrations of magnetism literally pull a plant's brain cells out through its roots.

Eating intelligent plants is a great way to stay healthy, but eating too many of them isn't, and some can have curious side effects. If you pile in too many moon nut leaves, then you can overdose on vitamin JX8, which temporarily makes you walk backwards in the style of a penguin.

Eat four or more bog trumpet seeds and this will cause an intense tickling sensation in your feet that will last for hours. It's also worth knowing that, although pickle plants might be tasty, overdoing them can lead to a nasty nasal discharge of bitter honey, tooth loss and bruising around the eyes.

On the moon, you will find intelligent plants that hiccup, burp, sneeze, cough, cry, croak and smell. This is normal. That's what plants do here. Some flowers read, write, think and dream, because the conditions on the moon allow them to.

A flower on the moon isn't just a pretty face, and we never pick one, unless given permission to do so by the flower itself. They don't normally mind if you ask, although some will want to know where they are going once picked. Remember that intelligent plants will speak to you, but they hardly ever strike up a conversation first.

Intelligent plants love being fed and don't need asking twice if they'd like seconds. Some plants like hair, cutlery and cricket balls, whereas others like batteries, space flippers and noise.

Most moon people feed plants on a Sunday when they go for a walk in the park. The jiggerjug plant is quite partial to bubble wrap, tangrams, bicycle pumps, and steak, although improper fractions and cheese feathers give them indigestion. Fern moon thistles love eating fairy wings and doorstops.

Tourists need to be aware that different plants eat different things, so it is always best to check first. Remember never to feed a daft plant to an intelligent plant, unless you want to be covered in clever sick.

The laughing plant is native to the craters of the Northern Hemisphere. This funny-looking plant has a 5ft stem with a circular yellow flower head and a red pair of lips. There are 24 different coloured petals that surround it. If you gently blow on the flower head, it starts to giggle and chuckle. When you stop, it stops. If it's a windy day, then it doesn't stop laughing.

Laughing plants release special hoot pollen into the atmosphere every day around mid-morning for about two hours. If you inhale some hoot pollen, then things start to happen to your body and there's not much you can do but enjoy the ride.

At first you start to grin and then you feel an itch in your nose, as if you are about to sneeze. This seems to stop, but quickly turns into an uncontrollable snorting attack for a full 90 seconds. You sound like a pig being tickled pink. This has everyone around you in stitches. Many of them laugh so much they split their sides open. If a laughing plant witnesses you having a snort attack, it laughs its head off and dies laughing.

The touchy plant is touchy by name and touchy by nature. It certainly isn't a touchy-feely plant. If someone touches a touchy plant, then it imitates dying and falls to a heap on the ground in a highly dramatic fashion, making all sorts of groaning noises as it goes. It then lies there until you have gone away, and afterwards will sprout up again, waiting for someone else to come along.

Even though each plant holds a sign saying, 'Do Not Touch', nearly everyone does just to see what happens. We get the feeling that touchy plants love overegging the pudding.

Along the roadsides across the moon you will find lots and lots of zibble plants. They have a 20cm stem with an orb that sits on the top about the size of a tennis ball made up of billions of tiny glowing bacteria.

The zibbles are great for lighting up the sides of the roads and pavements, because they glow when it gets dark and so everyone can see where they are going.

We know that plants on the moon grow faster to music. Research at the Moon Pod for Plant Perfection found that certain plants like different music, and the trick is to find the style that promotes growth.

They discovered that rock plants actually hate rock music, but will grow really well listening to aquagizzmuck. The giant hufferball plants of the Southern Hemisphere will almost double in size listening to sandbox maestro music, but will wilt if they listen to over 30 minutes of drudcrop.

Some plants grow so well to music that they produce bumper crops or grow extraordinarily large leaves. The flagtoe plant has been known to grow leaves over 80m after listening to music on a loop by Dark Light and Fluorescent Shadows. Its normal size leaves are just over 5m, so that tells you a lot. The flagtoe plant is full of vitamins and calcium, used to make shampoo, toothpaste and glass.

The carnivorous spit plant is one to watch out for, because it doesn't like admirers. To deter anyone thinking of getting close for a sniff, this beast of a plant spits an oily, slimy and smelly ball of mucus glob at you. They can spit very accurately.

The spit is made from the juices of digested frogs and rats it has caught. Get covered in that and you'll know about it, because it is rancid. A safe distance to look at a spitting plant from is about 15m, but even then, safety goggles are advised.

Gas plants are intelligent plants. They sense when the atmosphere on the moon is running low and needs topping up with essential gases. The atmosphere is normally great on the moon, but occasionally it starts to wane, so gas plants pump out plenty of gusto, zing and brio. If extra pep is required, then gas plants give it plenty of welly and the atmosphere soon packs a punch again and the mood of everyone is elevated a few stories higher.

Gas plants are particularly good at breathing in the harmful effects of splunge, a gas that artificial plants breathe out through the day. Splunge is a mixture of tired plastic and fake zest.

Number plant flowers have been described as out of this world by some people, despite being born on the moon. Their flower heads are made up of little cone-shaped buds that rotate anti-clockwise during the day and clockwise at night.

Pick a cone and gently squash it and you will find inside hundreds of tiny digits. These digits are data streams that have been sucked up by the plant's square roots from the soil. The data can be rubbed into your temples and they help you to see colours as numbers. The stem of a number plant flower is a 20cm thick spiral of stems that hold the 10kg flower head aloft.

Bookzip plants are found in hot zones and sit on rocks waiting for their prey. At first glance, they look like ordinary open books that someone has left behind after a spot of rock bathing. The glossy pages are covered in decorative fonts that attract moonflies – creatures that have an enormous reading appetite. The gloss is actually a gummy substance called mugwax, and anything that comes into contact with it normally meets a sticky end.

The book waits a couple of seconds and then closes with a bang. It then zips itself shut, so that nothing or no one can open it whilst it digests its meal. After about 30 minutes, the book then unzips, burps and opens up onto two fresh new pages, waiting for another reader.

Moonflies have been known to escape from bookzip plants. As soon as they land on a page, they immediately go into a flap. They flap so hard that they leave their legs behind stuck to the page. Moonflies that survive this ordeal find it hard to land anywhere after that, and spend the rest of their lives flying non-stop until they run out of flap and simply fall from the sky.

Bookzip plants don't stay in one location for too long, because moonflies get to know where they are, so they flap their pages and find another rock to sit on.

It has been found that plants across the moon adopt the regional accents and regional smells of the zone they belong to. Jack-in-the-Box plants appear to talk in the accents of people from the Vum Crater, and honk plants from the Wobble Crater do the same.

Scientists from the Plant Centre have recorded over 4,000 plant words and compared these to the words of moon people in both craters. The lilt and twang was a perfect match. Amazingly, both plants also mirrored the smells of their craters.

The Vum Crater smells of caterpillar breath and the Wobble Crater smells of toast. According to experts, moving some plants from one region to another can result in disaster, because the plants find it hard to understand each other and they start to wilt. Not all do, though, and there have been some very interesting mixing of accents over the years.

You've probably worked out by now that plants found on the moon are breathtaking. If you want to know more, then we recommend that you buy a book on moon plants and find out about plants with green fingers and mirrors for souls, plants that change colour in the wind, plants that can fly and plants that can only be seen in gravity hotspots. This will give you a good understanding of plant behaviour and will help you learn more about how to spot invisible plants.

Can you believe that some people on Earth think that the moon is actually a mirage and that the moon doesn't really exist at all? Others think that the moon is projected into the sky from a giant projector lamp from an island near the Arctic Circle. And then there are those people that think that the moon is like a giant CCTV eye in the sky.

Fortunately, billions of Earth people do believe in the moon, which is a relief. Unfortunately, there are a lot of superstitions about the moon which many people get confused. Below, you will find a collection of superstitions that are definitely nonsense, and some superstitions that are definitely not.

Moon superstitions that are nonsense

Some ideas about the moon just aren't true, and so we think we need to set the record straight so that you don't make a fool of yourself or get into trouble.

1. If you fish when there is a full moon, then your catch will taste of cheese. Nonsense. It will taste of wallpaper.
2. With respect to the nursery rhyme, 'Hey Diddle Diddle, the Cow Jumped Over the Moon', we can categorically say that the cow did not jump over the moon. It did a belly dance.

3. When there is a full moon, werewolves come out to play. No. People come out to play and ask, 'Where are the wolves, were they here or were they there?'

4. If you look at the moon without blinking, your teeth will fall out. False. You will sneeze three times.

5. The moon is a man. It isn't.

6. Stare at the moon too much and moonshine will make you drunk. No. The moonshine can make your knees smile.

7. The moon has a face nicknamed the Moona-Lisa. Not true. It waxes and wanes and has several nameless faces.

8. The moon wears make-up. No. That's made-up.

9. The moon and sun are brothers. Not quite. The moon is the sun's uncle's cousin's sister's great-great-great-not-so-great-granddad's brother.

10. If you dream of the number 13 when there is a full moon, then you will be lucky for 7 years. That's rubbish. You'll be lucky for 5.

11. If you sleep in direct moonlight, it will cause blindness and madness. Nope. It will cause baldness.

12. If you catch some moonbeams in a metal basin and wash your hands in it you, will be cured of warts. No, but wash your face in a moonbeam lotion and you'll look ten years younger.

13. A new moon is the best time to cut your fingernails. Rubbish. It's the best time to chew your toenails.

14. The moon disappears during certain days of the month. We don't go anywhere.

15. Seeing a new moon on a Wednesday means you won't be able to spell for toffee. No – it just means you won't be able to eat it.

16. If you see a new moon over your left shoulder then your food will taste of salt for a week. False. It will taste of yesterday.
17. Seeing a new moon over your right shoulder means you will have a bad neck and require hospitalisation. False. You will need cloud therapy.
18. If you hold hands with a monkey when there is a new moon then you will be richer than the Queen of Diamonds. No. You will meet someone with a heart of gold called Jack holding either a spade or a club.
19. If you see two full moons in one month, then you will have diarrhoea for eight hours. You wish, more like 36 hours. Take plenty of salt tablets.
20. Pregnant women who stare at the moon for two hours without blinking will give birth to a genius. False. They will just have sore eyes.
21. During a full moon, some people turn into werewolves. Nope. Some people turn over a new leaf, some turn the other cheek, and others turn left.
22. If you cut your hair between a jam-packed moon and a full moon, then your hair will never grow back. No. It will grow on your back.
23. More dog bites occur during a full moon than at any other time. This isn't true. They scratch more, they think more and they leave heavier deposits that are much harder to clean up.
24. No one can hear you shout on the moon. Really? Stand next to a Martian bacteria in Zone 34 and see how your ears react.
25. If you look in a puddle and you can see the moon's reflection, then a witch will visit you in your dreams. No. You will be visited by someone wanting to read the gas meter.

26. It is bad luck to see the moon reflected in an owl's eyes. No. In a cow's eyes, yes.
27. Robins can hear the dreams of moon people. This is why they are so friendly. Not quite. They can smell our dreams though.
28. It is rude to yawn in front of the moon. Not true. It is rude to yawn behind it, though.
29. If a frog enters your house when a cloud passes the moon, your bike chain will go rusty. No. It will dissolve.
30. If you whistle when there is a half moon, then your fishing rod will snap in two and your bread won't rise. Almost. Your fishing rod will dissolve and your bread will eat itself.

Moon superstitions that are fact

There are some ideas that have been rubbished as superstitious mumbo-jumbo, when in actual fact, they are true to life and need to be treated seriously, such as the following:

1. If you dream of a full moon and wake up to see one, then your toes will turn green for 100 days.
2. If you dream of a half moon and wake up to see one, then your hair will be impossible to comb for a month.
3. If you point to the moon in a storm, then your nose will drip sour honey for six days.
4. If you hold a black cat when there is a full moon, then a cow will kick your bathroom mirror.
5. If you look at the moon with one eye, your elbows will begin to itch.

6. If you wink at the moon and make a wish, your fingernails will cry.

7. If you are born on a full moon, then you qualify for 12 months free travel insurance (conditions apply).

8. If you walk ten times around a tree when there is a full moon, you will be able to climb inside its soul and hear what sort of bark it makes.

9. Never walk under a ladder when there is a full moon, as you will spend a lifetime tripping over.

10. Never cut your own hair on the moon or you will lose it forever.

11. Never look in the mirror when there is a full moon because your reflection will disappear.

12. Never move house in the moonlight or your new home will be haunted by moon dogs.

13. When it is a full moon if you gather a sprig of willow, a rusty key, a gold ring and a handkerchief, nothing will happen.

14. Look at a new moon on a Saturday and you will have bad wind for 48 hours.

15. Rob a bank on the third day of a full moon and your shadow will arrest you.

16. Look at the moon with a magnifying glass and you will see an image of yourself 30 years from now.

17. Chickens lay green eggs made of cheese when there is a full moon.

18. A cat born during a lunar eclipse will have its 9 lives multiplied by 7.

19. Going on a date during a solar eclipse is a bad idea.

20. If you walk under a ladder when there is a half moon, then all bad luck is cancelled.

21. If you smash a mirror when there is a full moon then your bad luck is shared with three people of your choice.

22. The moon has power over the water in human bodies, which is why people visit the toilet more when the moon is full: full bladder; full moon.

23. If you point a torch at the moon, then its light will go out.

24. If you go shopping when there is a full moon, then you will be short-changed.

25. Tie your shoelaces in the light of a full moon and your knots will be impossible to untie.

26. It's bad luck to draw a Jaswick wearing a hat when there is a half moon.

27. If a black cat runs towards you chased by a white butterfly, then you will see a blue moon in your dreams.

28. Dreaming that the moon is a jigsaw puzzle brings you good luck for 7 days.

29. A cow lifting its tail means a full moon is on its way.

30. If your right foot itches on a full moon, then you'll get a verruca on your left foot.

ETIQUETTE

When you visit the moon, you should be aware of a few rules about the way we do things here. Our manners might shock you, but try to keep an open mind and do what we do if you can remember to.

Meeting for the first time

When moon people meet for the first time, they burp in each other's faces and then lift and bend their left leg as high as they can. We maintain this position for about 30 seconds and then slowly lower the leg to the ground. To lower the leg before 30 seconds would be seen as very rude. Try to remember that the right leg should never be raised when greeting someone, as this is like telling them that their face smells of gob gas.

It is customary to gawp into someone's eyes for about 60 seconds before talking. This gives you a chance to search inside their mind for fingerprints, pick their brains and admire your soul in the reflection of their pupils.

When talking to family and friends, it is normal to stand with your arms in the air nodding and shaking your head and wiggling your hips. When we talk to strangers, we stand like a teapot with one arm on our hip and the other in the shape of a spout.

Not listening to every detail of a conversation is very important because we have to have our wits about us at all times. If we focus too much, this takes up valuable energy supplies. We also can't be bothered to listen that much because there are so many great things going on around us.

When we have had enough chatting, we take one step back and jump up and down until we run out of breath, can't get our words out and start giggling. Don't worry if someone walks off halfway through a story, as this is a sign of respect.

When chatting to each other, remember that constant interruptions are encouraged. Most topics get the thumbs up, but certain things should be avoided or a conversation is likely to crash and there may be casualties.

Try to steer clear of anything to do with the Moon Mirrors project, ghost cats, the number 9, boggle-wits or cheese fits.

It's also a good idea to reverse out of any conversation that looks like it might be heading towards talk about fig ships, headless owls, idea crematoriums, frozen sand, vowel surgery, glass ceilings or knee spots.

If it looks like a head-on collision between taboo subjects is on the cards, then our mouths will fill with hair. This stops words in their tracks and avoids a lot of bother.

Tourists who tempt fate by deliberately talking about a subject that is off limits will experience a foaming of the mouth. This leaves a taste of earwax and vomit for about 48 hours and generally stops people from running off at the mouth again.

If you are engaged in bibble-babble, chitter-chatter, gibble-gabble, prittle-prattle, or tittle-tattle, then eye contact must be maintained at all times. If you are talking rubbish, then try to keep at least one eye fixed on the person or people you are with.

Eyes that wander off and get distracted by passing people traffic drives us round the bend, so you are advised to read the Conversational Highway Code before you set off. You can buy a copy of this from the moonport or send off for a copy through sub-space.

Don't worry if the person you are talking to starts to imitate your voice. It is normal to adopt the accent of the person you are talking to, so that by the end of a conversation, you have swapped accents. This is great news if you like the voice you now have.

If you don't like it, then just find someone else to talk to and see if you like their twang. It's not uncommon for some people to have had fifty different accents by the end of the day. If you like your accent and would rather not swap it, then it's best to just keep quiet, listen and nod a lot.

Remember not to chat in a place where the wind factor is over 23, because your voice will more than likely end up on the other side of the moon. So many people have lost their voices this way. In fact, if you hear voices whilst touring the moon, try not to be spooked, because they are probably lost voices calling for their owners.

Unfortunately, lost voices spend most of their time wandering about the moon, get lost themselves and end up disappearing into cracks in the ground. Moon donkeys have been known to swallow lost voices, so don't be surprised to see people chatting to them, asking for directions.

Visiting friends

When visiting a moon person's house, don't knock on the door or ring the doorbell. Stand in the garden with your coat on back to front and hum. If no one hears you, then spin on the spot and whistle. If there is still no reply, then run away quickly until you are out of sight of the house.

Moon people consider it highly insulting to visit a friend without taking an even number of flowers. These have to be intelligent flowers with good qualifications. They can be any colour except schoolbus yellow. No one would be impressed if you turned up with a bunch of five diffy-drools, because these punch the air with bonfire smoke and stain your walls.

Before entering someone's house, it is good etiquette to post some rubbish through their letterbox and throw three eggs at their door. Never take your own shoes off. Your host will do that and then throw them into the back garden for you. A moon cat will then lick your feet, but remember to take your socks off first.

When offered a drink, remember to say no, because this means yes. As soon as you are given a drink, have a sip then spill the rest. No one will mind.

Eating out

Eating out is something you will do a lot of on the moon, and table manners are very important, so it is essential to learn the basics.

Before sitting down for a meal, stand behind your chair, pick your nose and then wipe your finger on the tablecloth or under the table. Some restaurants you visit will ask you to bring your own chairs, because they only provide the tables.

Other restaurants will request that you bring some stepladders with you, because their tables have exceptionally tall legs. It's not unusual to have a table with 8ft legs and if you don't have any stepladders, then you won't be allowed in, as the restaurants don't provide them and sharing is not permitted. If you do have them, then you climb to the top step and sit and enjoy your meal as you would normally.

The first course is always a pudding and this must be eaten with your little fingers. Slurping and chomping with your mouth open is considered good manners. Serviettes are not allowed.

Remember that after every course, you always swap chairs with the person sitting opposite you and burp as loudly as you can. If you are dining alone, then crawl under the table and sit opposite yourself.

The main course has to be eaten in silence. Anyone caught talking has to stand on their chair for 40 seconds with their arms folded. In this time, anyone else at the table is allowed to eat your food if they want.

It is considered polite not to eat everything on your plate, though. Always leave enough food for making a happy face on the plate at the end, so the chef can guess what you look like.

We end a meal by choosing something we don't like and forcing ourselves to eat it. To let the waiter know we have finished, we put our feet on the table.

When leaving the table, it is customary to bow and belch three times in the direction of the kitchen as a mark of respect for the food. The louder the better, as this indicates that you really enjoyed your meal.

When leaving the table, give one of the legs a good kick and tell the waiter the food was inedible and you will never be back again. This really means that you will return because the food was so good.

Although passing wind in restaurants is encouraged, this is not something you do in the street. Passing each other in the street involves a lot of staring, so don't be alarmed if you feel like people are looking at you. They are.

Out and about

Pointing is also something moon people do a lot of. It's not uncommon for half a dozen people to be pointing at someone as they walk by. Don't be put off by this, as it is actually a compliment.

When walking, remember not to swing your arms. You will never see a moon person do this and we'd prefer it if tourists didn't, either, as it makes the place look untidy. When shopping, always walk by the shop you want to go into and then suddenly change direction and run in.

If there is a queue to buy your shopping, then be prepared to queue backwards because that's the way we do it. To let someone know that the queue is moving forwards, we tap the shoulder of the person in front of us. We find this is a much better way to queue, because forward queuing tends to make people impatient as they can see too much.

Name calling

You may be called by many different affectionate names whilst staying on the moon. Get used to them.

For example, it wouldn't be uncommon to hear someone call you a pipnut, a washpopper, a sudnuffer, a jugpiddler, a dintpick or a guzzgrip.

These terms of endearment are spoken according to your age and what zone you are visiting. Don't think for a second that these are insults, because they aren't.

Insulting each other on the moon is an utter waste of time. If you call someone a rude name, your words will always boomerang and hit you in the face.

It works like this: imagine you are in a bad mood and you call someone a 'plapdunk'. This highly offensive word will fly out of your mouth at the speed of light, but just before it reaches your victim's ears, it spins neatly on its heels and heads back to smack you on the cheeks. The insult then writes itself on your forehead in special temple ink that lasts for 24 hours.

It won't budge or smudge, so don't bother trying to wash it off. Of course, everyone still does. Wearing a hat won't help, because the ink resists anything being pulled over it. To add injury to insult, your mouth fills with gob hair so that you can't speak for an hour and a quarter. After this time, the hair collects into a ball and spits itself out and runs away calling you a tweezer.

Gift-giving

Gift-giving is something you have to get right on the moon. You need to know that on the moon, a present is not the same as a gift. If you present someone with a present, then you normally wrap it up, give it to them and run off. We like to do this without revealing our identity. A disguise normally does the trick.

If you give someone a gift, you don't wrap it up, you download it. You see, gift giving is all about sharing something special that you have. For example, you might have a special gift for seeing inside the dreams of a banana, smelling sounds, or seeing upside down.

If you know a friend that would like a special gift, then you give it to them by sticking your finger in one of their nostrils and the gift is downloaded via gift shifting. After giving someone a gift, turn seven times in a clockwise direction and squeeze their cheeks gently with your left hand.

Behaving yourself

One thing that may surprise you about the moon is that we have no prisons. We don't have prisons because we don't have any criminals. You see if you are going to commit a crime on the moon, it is good manners to warn the Sky Police 24 hours before you have a chance to do anything reckless or silly.

The moon is the only place in the solar system where you can get arrested for committing the act of thinking about a crime. A heartfelt apology is normally enough to get you off the hook.

Earth tourists always seem to end up in trouble because they fail to read the *Moon Manual* from cover to cover on their journey from Earth.

The chapter 'An Eti-Kit Survival Guide' explains what you can and can't do, and we recommend that everyone familiarises themselves with its 6,205 page content.

Some examples are listed below:

- It is forbidden to walk down the street carrying bagpipes and dead wasps in a plastic bag.
- Try not to throw a tantrum. Roll one instead.
- You are not allowed to tie a slipper to a string and drag it through a park after dark.
- You must have a permit to feed a moon dog cheese.
- It is dishonest to faint in a library.

- If you butter someone up on the moon, you have to use margarine.
- Remember to wipe the smile off your face after laughing in Crater 29.
- Little white lies are not for common use. Big purple ones are more appropriate.
- It is illegal to threaten a smug lollipop.
- Tying yourself in knots is not allowed, but getting knotted is.
- Socks and handkerchiefs must be hung on separate washing lines, as they have been known to fight each other.
- Taking a moon lump to the cinema is taboo, but taking one to the theatre is widely accepted.
- Never look a moon fish or an optician in the eye.
- It is forbidden to fish in a talking moon puddle.
- Running after your dreams isn't widely practised, but walking after them is.
- Frightening carrots is seen as childish. Frightening radishes isn't.
- Blue ladybirds have the right of way and overtaking one is highly frowned upon.
- It is illegal to peel a klok in your hotel room.
- It is illegal to wear a false moustache, which can cause people to laugh in a library.
- You are not allowed to enter the Northern Hemisphere unless your clothes weigh more than 5kg.
- Avoid carrying a microwave near a gravity lamp.
- Never feed a moonpuffer expandable foam.
- Don't tap someone on the shoulder (unless queueing). Slap them in the face with a rubber chicken instead.

- Jumping into someone else's shadow is good manners.
- Avoid using a word with consecutive vowels in a public place.
- When doing someone a good turn, make sure the turn is always a right-hand turn and not a left-hand turn.

Don't worry too much if you end up committing a moon bungle. It's bound to happen.

Try to learn from your mistakes, though, as we do have a wide range of punishments available to us for repeat offenders and many of these involve tickling.

Holding hands

One thing it takes a lot of tourists time to get used to is street hand holding. Moon people will walk alongside each other as they go about their business and hold hands with complete strangers going in the same direction. You might think that's strange, but to us it would be strange not to.

If someone does walk with you and holds your hand, then just say hello and carry on walking. Try not to worry. If you want to make conversation with us, then by all means do. If you don't, then don't, because that's fine too. After a while, the person holding your hand will let go, depending on where they are going.

It's best not to overreact if someone walks alongside you and holds your hand, because you'll only make yourself look silly. The only rule is that adults cannot hand hold with children other than their own.

If you don't like the look of the person that holds your hand, then burp very loudly and they'll let go. Some tourists have plucked up courage to hand-hold with moon people by taking the initiative themselves. Moon people will respect you for this, as they know it isn't the norm on Earth.

When in Rome

Moon people are highly tolerant of others, but they respect visitors who try to live a moon way of life when staying. Those who continue to live by their own rules are soon asked to leave the moon and those who refuse are removed by the Sky Police. This hasn't happened since 1984.

Most moon people understand that it can be quite difficult to know all the do's and don'ts of moon life, because there are so many to remember and new rules are invented all the time.

If you don't do what you are supposed to do because no one has told you, then you can't really be blamed for doing it. New laws used to be posted on lampposts for everyone to read, until some bright spark made the law 'No reading notices on lampposts'. This caused chaos and the law was immediately changed, so that now dos and don'ts are just learnt from looking at each other and picking up vibes about whether something is right or wrong.

Try not to worry about what you are supposed to do. You'll soon work things out.

Moon sayings

It has come to our attention that the people of Earth have often used the moon in their everyday language and phrases when describing events and situations. If you are not familiar with these sayings already, then you will find the following collection fascinating and most probably useful when chatting about this and that – mostly that.

Once in a blue moon

Translation: very rarely
   Example: My brother lives in Crater 295, so I only get to see him once in a blue moon.

Over the moon

Translation: extremely pleased and happy
   Example: When she sent me a Saturn wasp trap and a box of Martian nuggets for my birthday, I was over the moon.

Ask for the moon

Translation: to make outlandish requests or demands for something
   Example: I only learnt the Neptunian musical scale this morning and now my teacher wants me to perform live in front of the Triton High Command. She might as well ask for the moon.

Moon something away

Translation: to waste time pining or grieving
Example: 'You have mooned half the year away crying about the Nidge-pipes you lost when digging for smoke in Zone 23. It's time to forget about them and move on.'

Moon about someone or something and moon over someone or something

Translation: to pine or grieve about someone or something
Example: 'Stop mooning about Knisper. Cats are always falling into space holes, but they always manage to get back home eventually.'

Promise the moon (to someone) and promise someone the moon

Translation: to make extravagant promises to someone.
Example: When the new job was advertised for Head of the Inner Circle, my boss promised me the moon. Talk about disappointed; the promotion went to someone from Zone 96 instead.

Hung the moon

Translation: To view or be viewed with uncritical or excessive awe, reverence, or infatuation.
Example: When my children were young, they thought I hung the moon. Now they have seen the light and realise that I can't draw Klap-jidges, I can't mend broken Buntles and I'm useless at changing a Dush-punnel.

Many moons ago

Translation: a long time ago
Example: I only have the faintest memory of seeing my first magnetic bubble storm. It all happened many moons ago.

Reach for the moon

Translation: to try to achieve something that is very difficult
Example: If you want success as an expert in space slug genetics, you have to reach for the moon.

It's all moonshine

Translation: empty, idle or foolish talk.
Example: We are perfectly safe. The idea that we will all be destroyed by the vibrations from a giant space burp in the next 5 years is all moonshine.

I know as much about it as the Man in the Moon

Translation: I know nothing
Example: I was at home making some nanoparticles with my hologram when the talking numbers were stolen. I know as much about it as the Man in the Moon.
Moon about *[see also mooner]*
Translation: to wander aimlessly and listlessly.
Example: From the moment Marc lost his job at The Lunar Halo Institute, all he's done is moon about watching rubbish on the rainbow screen all day.

To find an elephant in the moon

Translation: something that seems like a great discovery but isn't.

Example: Bing was delighted when he thought he had discovered magic plates in Zone 67. But he had found an elephant in the moon – they had been discovered 500 years earlier.

Casting beyond the moon

Translation: to make wild speculations

Example: We think that Earth will one day stop spinning and fall through space for 1,000 years before splashing into the Ocean of Infinity. We might be casting beyond the moon but anything is possible given what happened to Mercury last year.

Mooner

Translation: someone who wastes time.

Example: I asked him to clean the circumference of his crater ages ago, and he still hasn't touched it. He is such a mooner sometimes.

Moonlighting

Translation: to hold down more than one job, especially in hard times.

Example: Many Earth people end up moonlighting in order to afford the cost of travelling into space.

Something is not all moonlight and roses

Translation: it is not always pleasant

Example: Living on the East side of Mars might seem like a dream come true, but the weather there recently has proven it's not all moonlight and roses.

Moonstruck/Moonstricken

Translation: lost in fantasy, distracted or dazed with romantic sentiment
Example: Ever since Larissa's first meeting with Oberono, she has been moonstruck and unable to concentrate on her studies.

Mooncalf

Translation: a foolish person, a simpleton, a blockhead
Example: Even though it hasn't rained on Mars for three billion years, I think he is a mooncalf for going there without his umbrella.

Moonlight flit

Translation: to leave somewhere secretly at night, usually to avoid paying money that you owe.
Example: The bill for 6 moonshakes and 12 slices of mooncake was more than I had in my skyrocket, so I had no choice but to do a moonlight flit.

Moving from A to B is as simple as A, B, C on the moon. There are lots of ways to get around and we all have our favourites, depending on how hungry we are, what mind zone we are in, the time of day and the weather.

Moo-Moo Cabs

Your first travel experience on the moon is likely to be catching a moo-moo cab. These are self-steering, wheelless taxis that hover about half a metre off the ground and run on moon cow milk.

Earth people find it strange to take a ride in a car without a driver and worry about crashing every second of their journey. The point is that moo-moo cabs are 100% reliable and there has never been an accident in their 150-year history. Simply get inside a moo-moo cab, state your destination and the cab will take you there by the shortest possible route.

Payment is made by fingerprint, which is then charged to your moon account. In case you don't know how this works, your fingerprints are scanned when you arrive on the moon and anything you decide to purchase is then transferred to the moonport checkout desk. When you leave your fingerprints, the account tells us how much you have spent, and this is deducted from your Earth bank account automatically.

MDCs

To move from zone to zone on the moon, you can take a trip inside MDCs or magnetic directional corridors. These are twisting travel tubes of transparent glass that act like super motorways. They look like giant water tubes. To enter an MDC, moon people have to buy a ticket from special entry points called magna-gates. The tickets are magnetised and contain the information needed to get you to your destination.

When you step into a corridor, you scan your ticket on the side of the wall, confirm your intended destination and fall back. Don't worry, you won't hurt yourself, because a magnetic field catches you and transports you to where you want to go. You basically hover about 30cm from the glass in a horizontal position, and off you go.

When you buy your ticket, you can select your speed and whether you fancy a face-down or face-up position. The clever thing about an MDC is that you can enter any tube, anywhere and get to wherever you are going without having to change stations. There are no stations. There are no passenger collisions, either.

Clever Clogs

Whilst you are on the moon, you won't be able to resist trying clever clogs. They are a great way to get around, and you can hire them from shops displaying giant footprints.

Tell the shop assistant where you want to go and they will configure the clogs for you. They basically insert a navi-chip into each heel containing step-by-step directions to your destination. These chips effectively 'talk' to the clogs and literally walk you in the right direction. Of course, the only downside is that you have to leave your own shoes as a deposit.

Smart Shoelaces

People who don't want to hire clever clogs can buy smart shoelaces instead. They do the same thing, but look more stylish and you get to use your own shoes. Smart shoelaces contain pre-programmed directions that will take your feet to the places you want to go. They are self-tying and they change colour as you walk, so you know how near or far you are. They start off red, change to blue when you are about halfway and then give off green flashes when you are five minutes away.

Once smart shoelaces have been used on a particular journey, they cannot be reused, so it's a good idea to pay attention when you are on the move so you can remember the way for next time. Of course, moon people don't remember the route – not because they have poor memories, far from it. No, it's because they are extremely nosey and will spend most of their journey looking at what's happening around them, rather than learning the way.

After smart shoelaces have been used, they should be responsibly disposed of, in special tubes containing foot fudge. This dissolves the shoelaces and after a week, the fudge can be used to polish trees. It tastes like liquorice.

Mind Mapping

Some moon people are able to teleport themselves to different places by mind mapping. This involves reading and memorising a route from a map, closing your eyes, imagining yourself in a place, opening your eyes and actually finding yourself there.

You would imagine this would be a popular way of travelling, but it isn't, because you don't get to see any sights, and moon people love sightseeing. There are problems with ending up in the wrong zone sometimes, as some people use out-of-date moon maps. This can be embarrassing if you are dressed for a swim and end up at an ice zoo!

DDDs

An unusual way to get around the moon, at least for Earth people, is to use a Doppelganger Directional Device, or a DDD, as we call them. These 4D holograms can be disconcerting, and they are not for everyone.

A hologram centre will set you up. They scan your whole body in a special multi-coloured room. After about five minutes, an exact replica of you walks through a door and waits for your instructions. The DDD will only respond to instructions that relate to directions.

So, if you said, 'Please take me to Zone 14, Street 56' then the DDD would lead the way by walking about 3m in front of you and get you there safely.

Their job is to get you to where you want to go. They are very reliable, as they are programmed with every known destination on the moon.

You do need to be location-specific, though. Ask a DDD to take you shopping and they will just look back at you and smile. They don't speak. Earth people find it incredibly spooky to see themselves projected like this. You can even walk through yourself if you want. You won't feel anything, though, as the DDDs are made up of coloured light.

DDDs can malfunction from time to time, which puts some people off using them. Sometimes they walk too fast and get so far ahead you lose sight of them. Occasionally they walk backwards and head back to the hologram centre. Now and then, they will just disappear right before your eyes.

Their most common fault is stopping to look in shop windows that you are not interested in. This can be embarrassing because you end up shouting at your DDD, trying to get it to move and show you the way. To an observer, you can imagine how this looks.

Trouser Walk

If you have plans for taking a trip to another part of the moon and want to be prepared, then just send your trousers ahead of you. Most hotels offer a trouser walk service, and it's well worth trying.

Select the trousers you want to wear on the day you want to travel. Place them in a bag with a note inside for the hotel maid saying where it is you want to go. When you are at breakfast, the maid will put a belt around your trousers, plug a destination chip into the buckle and the trousers will walk the trip there and back for you.

The next day, your washed and ironed trousers will be left in your room, ready to wear. Put your trousers on and they will take you to your destination when you are ready. They effectively learn the route for you.

This is a popular choice for many people, although trousers have been known to go missing when sent out on a journey, never to return. We think that splodge-nippers take them. These are irritating little creatures about the size waste bins that originate from one of Jupiter's moons. We put up with them even though they are pains, because they are employed to clean moon sewers. We have no idea why they steal trousers and no one dares go into the sewers to find out.

Runnipede Train

Another way to get about is to take a runnipede train. These are pretty much like Earth trains, but the carriages don't have wheels. They have lots of very supple metal legs that run at speeds faster than a hummingbird can flap its wings. Not only are runnipede trains tyre-less – they are also tireless. Their service is a light time and a nighttime operation and they are ruthlessly efficient.

They are never late and they don't like their passengers being late, either. They can also be rude if you are slow getting on and off a train, because it threatens their punctuality. If you do dilly-dally, then you are quickly ejected by a helpful member of the train crew.

You would imagine that runnipede trains are popular with moon people. They are – but not with everyone because the trains have a 'no talking' policy in all their carriages and that includes telethapy. Talking is not seen as an efficient use of time and the hot air can make the cabins too warm.

Mulch Roads

If this mode of transport doesn't float your boat, then why not try the mulch roads we have on the moon? These are fast moving strips of safety rubber tarmac that move nonstop between places. All you have to do is climb aboard and let the road drive you to wherever you want to go to. The spongy road surface means that travel is perfectly safe and falling over is not a problem.

These marvellous conveyor belts are well used, but some don't like them because their speed limit is restricted to 15gph (gunkanigs per hour). That might not get you to where you want to go fast enough. There are plans to increase the speed of mulch roads to 16gph, which is good news, and this might encourage more people to travel. We honestly don't know why Earth people still put up with static roads anymore. We haven't had a traffic jam for over 300 years.

Sky Cat

One of the most exciting ways to get around the moon is by sky cat, but to do this you have to belong to the Sky Police. The sky cats are regenerated sabre-toothed tigers from Earth that have been 'techdapted' for life above the moon as rapid response space craft.

These incredible beasts can move at sickening speeds when they need to, but they mostly cruise above us without a sound and make sure we are safe at all times.

You would of course be extremely lucky to see a sky cat, because they have cloaking devices that make them invisible. They only uncloak when there is an emergency to attend, and there hasn't been one of those on the moon for about 50 years.

The only way you'll get to ride a sky cat as a human is if you are in trouble with the Sky Police. A word of warning: don't even think about it, because sky cats aren't big fans of jokers.

Sky Wires

If you feel up to it, then magnetised wire walks could be for you. Certain locations on the moon are connected by sky wires, because the terrain below is protected. Footprints are banned in many parts of the moon.

Sky wires hang over the land, held up by 200m high sky poles. The wires are magnetised, which means if you are wearing magnetic boots, then you can walk along them and enjoy some of the most unspoilt landscapes on the moon.

Walking a tightwire might not be everyone's idea of fun, but for funambulists, it's the only way to travel. You shouldn't worry too much about coming off, either, as no one has ever fallen off a tightwire. The magnetism between shoes and a tightwire is so strong you could even walk upside down on a wire and not come off.

Interestingly, the height isn't what puts many people off from using sky wires - it is the Moon Lunz. These pesky birds really know how to make a nuisance of themselves. As you are walking, they sit on your head; they walk across your shoulders, and they hover in front of you and pull ridiculous faces. They also like to dive bomb you and leave a deposit or two if they can hit their target.

Flying Dominoes

If you fancy getting around the moon on something a bit different, then perhaps giant flying dominoes are for you. The great thing about this form of travel is that you have 28 different tiles to choose from, all made from soapstone. The hollowed out spots on the tiles act as seats and we call them bum-pips.

The tiles have a different number of bum-pips on them to accommodate the needs of all passengers. If you want to travel alone, then the tile 'blank – one' is the one for you. If you are in a group of twelve, then tile 'six – six' is just perfect. There are tiles for all family sizes, so we have something to suit everyone. The blank tile without any seats is used as an emergency tile and bum-pips can be added as required. The bum-pips are popular because they have transparent bottoms, which mean you can see underneath you as you fly.

Some people say that flying dominoes are similar to magic carpets, but they aren't really. Magic carpets have a poor safety record, as they tend to malfunction after 1,000 flights. Some carpets have inexplicably come to a sudden halt above gravity hotspots, flipping their passengers into orbit.

Magic carpets also need a lot of cleaning. They tend to absorb smells and unpleasant odours from passengers and their pets and they stain easily. They also go mouldy underneath. Flying dominoes have none of these problems, which explains why magic carpets are such a rare sight these days. Flying teabags are also something you are unlikely to see, unless you visit the Museum of Movement in Crater 430.

Hollow Asteroids

One way to get a feel for the moon and all that is on offer here is to fly into orbit and travel around the moon. You can do this by travelling inside hollowed out asteroids as these protect you from the space debris and rock showers that revolve around us.

Asteroids have triple-triple glazed windows and the interiors are surprisingly comfortable and contain all mod-cons. Hollow asteroids are available to hire in different sizes and are the perfect way to see the moon and get your bearings before exploring. They are ideal for moon parties.

To get to the Hollow Asteroids take a gravity train to Crater 500, where the Orbit Catapult is located. Once you have chosen a suitable asteroid, you will then be flung into the space surrounding the moon to weave in and out of the 13 moons that orbit us. This is about 44,000 mickahoops above the moon's surface. Remember to go to the toilet before orbiting as there are no facilities on board. It might be an idea to bring your own bucket.

Sky Stones

You could of course try our sky stones. These are like stepping-stones, and sit about 100m up in the air, above some of the protected parts of the moon.

The sky stones aren't actually stones, but triangular puddles of kaleidoscopic water that can be stepped in without falling through.

To access the sky stones, you climb a ladder and chose a route when you reach the top. You might feel a bit nervous stepping into a puddle at first, but they won't let you down if you believe in them and trust them. They are about 8cm deep and about the size of Martian postage stamps. Don't worry, that's big enough to swing a cat in. To step onto another stone requires a leap of faith, even though the stones aren't that far apart.

If you were to miss your footing, then you wouldn't fall to the ground. For one thing, the moon's gravity isn't going to pull you down in a hurry, because it's far too chilled for that. Secondly, the square puddles stretch to make sure you don't go far. Sky stone routes zigzag around large territories and are perfect for seeing bits of the moon that are otherwise out of bounds.

Is anyone at home?

You could be mistaken for saying, 'Do moon people exist at all? They just don't seem to be around.' You can travel for hours without seeing a soul, and you begin to wonder whether you've had a wasted trip. Visitors to Earth used to think the same thing, too, when travelling for hours across empty deserts. The point is, moon people are here, there and everywhere – you've just got to know where to find them.

Try looking skywards around midday. Loads of moon people like to stop what they are doing around this time and just go for a float in the sky. It helps us to clear our minds. That's right – moon people can float. Some call this flying, but it isn't really, because we don't have wings.

When we float, we mostly do this alone. We stand in the sky quite motionless, not bumping into each other, or disturbing anyone. Everyone respects everyone else's space. After five minutes, moon people will look at the people next to them, smile and return to the moon's surface, and then carry on doing what they were doing.

Earth people normally stand and stare when this happens and can often develop bad necks as a result. Even after moon people have floated back to the moon, Earth people still look skywards, necks back and mouths open wide. This is the best time for flies to fly in. This is also the best time to tie someone's shoelaces together without them knowing. Sky floating can turn into sky strolling simply by walking. Airborne moon people like to sky stroll on Sundays and the air can get quite crowded above big cities.

MOON THINGS NOT TO MISS

You will have so much to do and see on the moon you will need to plan carefully.

One place everyone seems to head for is the Ziggy Crater. This is home to the tallest structure on the moon - The Gug, a 1600m atmos-scraper. This hulking building has 500 floors and a viewing platform at the top, from where you can see the 13 black moonlets that orbit the moon - the Baker's Dozen. These amazing moons cannot be seen from Earth. They are about 1/6 the size of the Moon itself and orbit in harmony with us. 12 of the moons orbit clockwise whereas the 13th moon moves anti-clockwise and interweaves between the other 12. The distance between the 12 moons correspond to the intervals of the scale in music.

If you've always wanted to step back in time then you might want to try a holomatrix experience in Zone 28. Here you will find the the Moon Corridor of Yorick, home to 1,500 holomatrix theatres, built around the circumference of the Yorick Crater. Pay to enter any historical period for an hour at a time and change the course of history! The theatres replicate the people, sights, sounds, smells and movements of any period on Earth. For the time that you are inside a theatre, everything is real!

Of course, it's not possible to see everything the moon has to offer on a short trip, and we don't suggest you try it. What follows is a selection of the moon's best bits, as voted for by Earth visitors last year. We recommend you pick a handful and explore.

1. The Listening Mirrors

If you visit the Copper Palace in Zone 50, be sure to find the Magna-Soda Pool. Above this vast swimming pool hang 100 listening mirrors. Climb into the pool, find a mirror and then lay back to see and hear anything on Earth. Simply name a place or person and your listening mirror will show you what you want to see and let you listen in as if you were there in person. Advance reservations are essential and visits to the pool are restricted to 50 minutes.

2. The Lucian Tower

If you are after surrealism, then this is the place to find large servings of it. The Lucian Tower is an 800m cobalt tube covered in eyeballs and long hair. The hair goes from top to bottom and when the wind blows, it reveals its eyeballs. The inside of the tube contains impossible dreams, half-forgotten memories, dissolving walls, swallowing floors, and rotating rooms full of the bizarre and peculiar. Check out the gift shop in the underground temple where you can buy collapsed bags of nonsense. The Lucian Tower is in the outlands of Zone 215.

3. The Purple Waters of Chacma

The Collins Crater in Zone 98 is the largest on the Moon. This enormous bowl is filled with purple warm water and gives off a mesmerising purple mist. Go swimming there and you might be lucky enough to see the purple-skinned moon baboons. These wonderfully gentle creatures walk on the water as if it was land. They emerge from the depths singing, whistling and waving, and after a while, disappear back into the water again, smiling as they go. You never know when they will appear and no one knows how many there are in the water. The Purple Waters are home to the flying dish fish and this is the place to have a go at pole sitting and compete against one of the locals.

4. *The Spinning Plate of the North*

Located in the Northern Ceiling is a spinning titanium plate the size of a dinner plate that floats about 20m above a small pool of golden-brown fog. The plate spins continuously and every hour gives out three flashes and turns itself inside out. Hundreds of sparkling dust particles escape and climb high into the atmosphere. These form the shapes of birds and then fly away into space. Head for Crater 60.

5. *The Laughing Stalactites of Cave Nebra*

Climb deep into the moon, 7km below the surface, and take a tour through a 40-acre, awe-inspiring cave containing thousands of laughing luminous stalactites, some as big as 15m. It's not a place for the faint-hearted, as the echoes of laughs from distant stalactites can be unnerving and the cavern is bathed in an eerie blue glow which the stalactites produce. It is rumoured that ghost vowels roam the cave and shoot firecrackers into the darkness to scare tourists. Tickets to Zone 300 have to be pre-booked.

6. *Mount Draw*

Nestled in the lap of the snow-capped moon ranges and silver valleys of Zone 28 is Mount Draw, a place where things move uphill and defy gravity. Stand at the foot of Mount Draw and watch streams move uphill. Place marbles on the ground and watch them slowly climb the slopes and bounce into the distance. Take off your walking boots and watch them take a hike, too!

7. The Skies of Dreams

In the remote moon lands of Zone 1, you will find very little on the ground except moon dust. Look up, though, and you will see giant rotating rainbow cylinders that reach into space. These magical tubes of colour stand proud like pillars holding up the universe. Lay on the ground and let your dreams wash over you.

8. The Dancing Tornadoes of Luna 2

The Luna 2 Sea is an enormous body of water located in between Zones 34 and 35. From the coastline, you can witness amazing sand storm tornadoes that dance on the surface of the sea. The tornadoes measure 100m in height and are too difficult to count. They have never been known to hit land. Boat trips are forbidden.

9. The Guri Graveyards

Located on the site of the first Mars rocket to hit the moon, Guri is the eerie graveyard home to thousands of red bones. No one can explain why there are so many or why they are strewn so far and wide, but they are a sight to behold. The bones have never been disturbed and visitors are not permitted to take photographs. Zone 227.

10. *The Mirror Mirages of Mixy*

Mixy is a coastal town in Zone 8. Here you can see – if your eyes will let you – mirror mirages of castle cities. The mirages appear on the surface of the water, upside down, in the air, and underwater. They disappear if you approach them, but if you keep your distance, then you can marvel at these futuristic cities and their amazing castles. Children are not allowed to participate in the underwater visits.

11. *The Moon-Ogler*

The Moon-Ogler is the moon's infrared telescope and it is our eye into space. The Moon-Ogler has been able to see spinning ring galaxies, ghost galaxies, yellow hole storms, and the Zip solar system with its amazing 12 suns. Thanks to the Moon-Ogler, we now know that there are multiple universes, each with their own separate histories and futures. Zone 0, Street 1.

12. *Cafe Moonglow*

After all this sight-seeing then it's time for a rest, and what better place than Cafe Moonglow, a large, buzzing meeting place at the back of the Fishbowl library. Cafe Moonglow offers fresh lunar food, amazing moonshakes, and the best chimney cakes you have ever seen. They also serve puddings that sing! You will find that the waiting staff are rude and will shout at you, but don't be offended because this is done on purpose and is part of the attraction. This is the coolest place on the moon to spend a few hours people-watching. Moon cafés come in all shapes and sizes but Cafe Moonglow takes the biscuit. Zone 0, Street 2.

The Moon's climate is extreme. It's also a bit barmy. Where else in the solar system will you see upside down fire rainbows, dry rain and embarrassed wind?

Is there another place this side of the Ragged Space Curtain where you will see a storm in a teacup, column rain, zero-gravity green ball-lightning, and happy clouds?

We only really have one season on the moon and that's the silly season, so the clothes you pack for your stay here should reflect that.

Storms in teacups are quite common in the zones, and they can be quite disruptive depending on how much sugar you take and where you are sitting. They can happen at any time, in any place and to anyone.

The storms are like mini-tornados and probably only measure about 5cm in height, but they still pack a punch with wind speeds close to 30mph. That's a lot for a teacup.

So, you might be in a cafe and you order a cup of tea. You add a couple of sugars, give it a stir and take a sip. All is well.

Then the tell-tale signs start.

The saucer starts to shake and the cup begins to wobble and before you know it, your tea has developed an attitude problem. The tea tornado soon knocks things flying and races across the table, tossing everything in its path skywards. Within seconds, it's all over and the tempest just stops in its tracks and the hot tea just splashes to the floor, or if you are really unlucky, all over your lap.

The ferocity of a storm in a teacup seems to be related to the number of sugars you take and the number of stirs you administer. Adding milk seems to make no real difference.

There is one way of stopping the tornado and that is removing the saucer, but you have to be quick. Why do we bother with saucers, then? Well, a cup without a saucer is like a foot without toes; it's part of the uniform.

You might be wondering why we bother with tea at all, but you have to remember that moon people love tea and besides, a storm in a coffee pot is so much worse.

By far the nicest weather we get can be found in Zone 49. It's the sort of place you can wear a T-shirt all day and just take your time. It's warm in this district, but not muggy like it is in Zone 6, where the humidity clogs your salt shaker, swells your ankles and makes your feet stink.

No, Zone 49 is the sort of place where the temperature suits everyone, and where suits are definitely not needed. You will find that life in this area is more laid back – it's a place where many moon people themselves choose to come for a holiday.

The clouds above Zone 49 are all cloud 9 types, and none of them can be bothered to rain. So if you are feeling genuinely under the weather, then Zone 49 is the weather to get yourself underneath.

Most moon people are under the weather because that's where the weather comes from – above. We do get a bit of weather knocking around our ankles from time to time, but that tends to be low-level wind activity or pavement sparks.

Some of our weather is related to volcanic activity. When a moon volcano erupts, it produces thousands of mottled blue eggs, which float on the surface of a warm green larva.

Moon larva is great for paddling in, although it can dye your feet and tickle your toes. It is also great for helping eggs to hatch. When a volcano egg breaks open, a translucent bubble the size of a ping-pong ball emerges. This slowly climbs into the atmosphere.

When the bubbles reach 18,000m, they pop and fall as fandango rain, which is pink and warm. This is dancing rain and makes excellent drinking water. Dancing rain falls twice a day and helps keep the moon clean, the ground nourished and feet happy.

The coldest part of the moon is the Equator – a 200km wide band of frost that stretches around the moon like an ice-belt. Some moon people cannot live near the Equator because they are afraid of widths and the Equator is a pretty wide part of the moon. It is cold here and blue snow falls for about six months of the year. The snowflakes are 30cm wide, 8cm deep and taste delicious.

Snowstorms are things to watch out for if you are in this neck of the woods. If you see a heavy-looking cloud about 1km wide sitting still above you, then move, quickly.

These clouds as known as dumps, because they dump enormous amounts of snow in one go, not as individual flakes, but as one giant ball. You'll know when a dump is about to let go because it sends pulses of red and green light around its circumference and then just opens up, unleashing an almighty ball of blue snow about 250m wide. Whatever is under a ball of snow this big has a

100% chance of being flattened, which is why we recommend you stay indoors.

Snow is something you won't see much of, except in the ice-belt, but we do get horizontal snow showers from time to time, which fly about 3m above ground. This snow normally flies up and down roads in long lines going back and forth, not really doing very much apart from going nowhere fast. Then it suddenly stops and just collapses on the ground in one big heap.

The snow is always very considerate, though, as it is self-cleaning and will move itself off roads and pavements so we are not inconvenienced.

A surprising number of people choose to live in the ice-belt Equator because they love making ice sculptures and they enjoy the cold. The Ice Park is the place to see sky taps, rockets, a roller coaster, pyramids, an ice scraper and a dozen ice replicas of Earth through the ages. This is the place where exclamation mark icicles hang from the sky, so you'd be mad not to visit.

You've probably gathered that the Equator is a bit on the chilly side, which might put you off. People who are born in the ice-belt know no different, and they find it strange when people from other parts of the moon complain how cold -90G is.

The hottest parts of the moon are the Northern Ceiling and the Southern Floor, otherwise known as the Tip-Tops. Here you will find large parts of the land covered in thousands of iron discs with holes in their centre.

As the ground heats up through the day, the iron discs rise and swell into doughnuts. These float above the ground and by mid-afternoon leak lingo-lingo jam everywhere. The jam is licked up by moon cats, who love the metallic taste. We hate it, though, which is why we don't touch the stuff.

Gradually the iron doughnuts float back to the ground and then shrink into iron discs for the night. They grow umbilical cords that reach into the soil and feed off the sugar of insect dreams. This process is repeated every day and is quite a sight.

Earth tourists tend to head for the Tip-Tops when they arrive, but they underestimate how hot it is there and soon end up in the moon zones where they can breathe normally. We have never understood why so many Earth people enjoy burning their skin. To us, this is a very odd thing to do.

The Northern Ceiling is home to a surprising number of creatures who can tolerate extreme heat, such as the hopping moon tortoise, cleft worms and fezzers. These creatures tend to be quite shy around moon people, but they are not backwards in coming forwards when around tourists.

The Southern Floor is exactly the same as the Northern Ceiling in every respect and exists as a parallel universe in its own world. Here you will find the same weather, the same creatures, the same teabags, the same everything. The only difference is that the flavour of gravity is slightly sweeter in the South Floor compared to the North.

Moon zones all have their own freak weather systems and within these zones, many craters also have their own unique weather glitches. This is always awe-inspiring for tourists new to the moon. In fact, some Earth tourists visit the moon just for the weather, and will tour every moon zone without paying much attention to anything else.

A lot of the weather we experience can't really be explained by anyone. It just happens. We used to have weather experts employed to have their heads quite literally above the clouds, but they were always quiet before a storm and kept getting things wrong. We find it's better to just let nature do the talking now.

On Earth, people say that every cloud has a silver lining, which we find strange. On the moon, our clouds have yellow linings, green linings and blue ones, too. We also have clouds of suspicion and superstitious clouds. These normally gather over Cloud-Cuckoo Land in Crater 98.

The moon is blessed with lots of clouds, including pyramid clouds, spherical clouds, kite-shaped clouds, and star-shaped clouds.

Lots of interesting things tend to fall from moon clouds. For example, a shower of yellow fluffy mice vomiting peas fell on the moon in 1578. We think they may have been blown over in a solar backwind from Venus, but then again, they might have been living in our atmosphere for years, and they just fell through a cloud hole.

Where they disappeared to we haven't a clue. Although there have been sightings of large furry yellow mice the size of small cars in the Tip-Tops, riding on the back of tortoises. If these reports are true, then they've grown, and we really should be more concerned about their plans for future growth.

Other odd things to have rained down on us over the years include compasses, space sponges, artificial legs and fluorescent worms. All clouds can be lifted by sky cranes if we don't like the look of them.

Rainfall on the moon isn't quite the same as rain on Earth. In craters less than 50 miles wide rain falls upwards from inverted clouds. This eventually falls to the moon as a special dry type of rain, so you'll never get wet.

In craters over 50 miles wide, wet, red rain tends to fall in cylindrical columns, which mean that there are always dry patches you can step into to avoid a soaking. Each rain column is about 2m in diameter.

Although there are lots of rain columns that can fall at the same time, you could dash from dry patch to dry patch with a bit of nifty footwork and a healthy slice of luck. Alternatively, you could just stand in a dry patch and admire the columns until they stop pouring. This is sailing too close to the wind for some people, though, because the columns have been known to move.

Some people prefer to stand under a rain column because it's like having an enormous power shower. Some moon people have been known to produce a rainbow when they get wet. It arcs over the shoulders, coming out of one armpit over to the other.

When we say it's been raining cats and dogs on the moon, we mean it. Hairless dogs called Bungtons and toeless Hell-cats fall from the skies in large numbers in Zone 24 almost every day, and if you are in the area then it's wise to take cover. Not because they splat all over the pavements. No, they are too clever for that. They parachute in.

Wind is something to respect on the moon. You can't normally see it, unless you are in Zone 33, and to actually see it in the flesh will almost certainly put the wind up you. Once you've seen the wind, you never really want to see it again.

Go and have a look for yourself and see what we are talking about. Don't pull faces there, because if the wind sees you – then it will change direction and you are left with the face you pulled. This is why so many people visiting Zone 33 wear a mask, because the shock of seeing the wind for the first time isn't the look you want to be wearing for the rest of your life.

If you'd rather not risk having a change of face, then stay away from Zone 33 and all half-price offers to go there.

If you live in Zones 18-20, then you will be used to seeing pinball lightning. These magnificent blue and white orbs of wonder fly out of nowhere, and as soon as they hit an object, they bounce from pillar to post until they get tired and then explode in an orange flash of glory. They vary in size from a football to a pea, they make no noise (until they explode) and they don't smell – much!

They do, however, hurt if you come into contact with one, especially if you have your mouth open at the time. Anyone hit by a pinball is likely to be knocked into the air and knocked out for a week, unable to remember their own name. There have been cases where some people have woken up with a completely new set of memories, orange skin and the ability to speak to frogs.

Fortunately, ball strikes can be predicted. If moon dogs suddenly start eating blue grass like there is no tomorrow and the moon mountains start to whistle to each other, then it's time to close your windows, your doors and your mouth.

Pinball lightning strikes are spectacular to watch, especially if they hit more than one object. There is a stretch of lunar road that is 50km long that contains over 20,000 lamp lines. If a lightning ball hits one of these, then it bounces between them from one side of the road to the other in an insane frenzy.

You might be wondering whether it's worth bringing your umbrella to the moon. Not really. We don't trust them and they have a reputation for arguments. If you do bring an umbrella, you will be required to keep it in a locked cabinet at all times for the duration of your stay.

Weathers come and go on the moon and change like the wind. We are never quite sure what we will get from one minute to the next.

Something unusual normally slips through a space crack from another galaxy and gets pulled in by our gravity. We've had triangular clouds that squirt dry ice helixes. We've had balls of steam that rise and fall but never touch the ground. We've had ghost rain from mirage clouds. And some days we have no weather at all, as our moon mirrors have been able to reflect the weather back to where it came from.

FOOD

Have you ever wondered what people eat on the moon? You've probably heard on the solar system grapevine that the moon is made of cheese. Well, that is entirely true, but we don't eat it. This is because it tastes like noggled chalk and has no nutritional value. It has no export value, either, which is a relief.

So what do we eat? Our food is exquisite, bordering on ridiculous. Let's start with some of the things we grow.

Clizzpippers are root vegetables similar to Earth carrots, except they aren't orange and they don't help you see in the dark when eaten. They will help you to see in the dark if you *don't* eat them, though, because they glow a shocking pink at nighttime.

If you eat clizzpippers regularly, they can help you levitate. Given the right conditions, clizzpippers grow to about 3m and are packed full of goodness, particularly snish nectar, a juice rich in anti-ageing molecules. They basically keep you looking fresh-faced and wrinkle-free. To benefit from their properties, you do have to eat a whole one, which can be time-consuming. Clizzpippers are grown by everyone everywhere, because everywhere, everyone wants to stay looking their best.

Unfortunately, Earth people and clizzpippers don't get on that well, because they have the opposite effect. We found that when Earth people tried them, their skin would start to sag, making them look considerably older.

It amazes us that Earth people still eat them, despite warnings not to.

You'd think the smell and taste would be enough to put people off, because Clizzpippers whiff of burning rubber and have a stale, sweaty slipper flavour. We find this quite agreeable and gentle on the stomach, but we've seen far too many Earth people in distress to know that clizzpippers aren't their cup of tea.

Crunkleflobs are root vegetables, too, but much smaller than clizzpippers. They are round, bright blue and the size of a golfball. They also have their own nervous system and can feel pain, so they have to be handled with care when being picked. Pull them out of the ground too hard and they will give out a roar similar in power to the growl of a moon bus that has lost its exhaust pipe. Crunkleflob roars are strong enough to knock you off your feet, so it's worth picking them with care.

They grow wild in moon deserts and can be quite hard to find. Moon people used to pick crunkleflobs themselves, but teams of land heptapusses from Saturn do this for us now.

Cooking crunkleflobs is a crime, which is why they have to be swallowed raw. This isn't easy, as they are quite furry, so avoid rolling them around your mouth as they can tickle and cause you to choke. When a crunkleflob enters your stomach, it bursts into hundreds of tiny crunkleflobs. These pinhead-sized little wonders help to fight infections, bugs and bacteria and keep moon people fighting fit. They really are quite amazing, but they do have one side effect that can be embarrassing. They give you gas so they are better eaten alone and indoors. Never eat one in a lift or in a swimming pool.

By far the most unusual food we eat is a buzzfunk. This star-shaped fruit grows inside a floating copper sphere about 1km above the moon. When it is ready to hatch, the copper sphere unfurls like a flower, and the buzzfunks parachute to the moon. On their way down, they cook themselves, so that they are ready to eat by the time they land. They can be quite hot after landing and a few people have had their fingers burnt, so always wrap a buzzfunk in its own parachute until it has cooled down.

Buzzfunks have a crispy outside, but bite into one and they melt in your mouth. This makes your taste buds dance the bumbumba, and that's quite a dance. Some people think they taste like camel meat and others think they are more like woodpecker feet in flavour, but they remind others of flamingo tongue. Everyone is different, and whatever the taste, people love eating them.

They are particularly good for Earth people's ears, as they stop wax from building up and clogging sound tunnels. Most moon people eat them for the energy hit. One buzzfunk is the equivalent of 50 bananas, and that keeps us going for quite a while. Even so, we always eat more than one buzzfunk because, as you know, moon people are always on the go and pretty restless.

Buzzfunks always parachute into the moon at the same time every day, which is just before 6 a.m. This is quite a sight and well worth getting up early for. They are best eaten fresh and are good to go for a good three hours after landing. Any later than this and buzzfunks start to steam and turn to liquid mush. Waiting in the wings are moon foxes, who waste no time in lapping them up.

Moon people are quite partial to fangowinks. In appearance they are not unlike jumbo-sized robins with small heads and hair like busbys. Fangowinks are cute, and so we don't eat them. Well, not quite – we eat part of them. You see, we are really only really interested in their curly toenails. These smell like furniture polish and are surprisingly very appetizing, but only when fried in liquorice oil. If eaten raw, they can make your earlobes tingle and will turn the palms of your hands yellow. Some people choose to eat them that way because they like yellow hands and itchy ears.

Fangowink toenails are full of a sort of sandy marmalade and they have a taste similar to otter droppings. A word of warning, though – frying toenails should only be attempted by a skilled moon chef. If they are fried too quickly, they bray like a donkey, which can be distressing for all concerned. If they are fried for too long, then they will sing Christmas carols backwards, which can be even more upsetting. Learning to fry them at the right temperature takes about two years.

Fangowinks have no particular nutritional benefits – they just make you feel good. They release a chemical in your cheek muscles that makes you smile like a Cheshire cat that has found a field of four-leaved clovers made of cheese.

Each crater on the moon has its own traditional food, with delicacies that might surprise you. The Niptin Crater is famous for its microchips served in big bowls and eaten like rice. They are quite crunchy, a good source of health and delicious with a magnetic sauce.

If you are wandering around Snack Street in the Peenix Crater, then you may see street vendors selling live zab larvae on sticks. These are eaten like a kebab and taste a bit like moon crab.

In Crater 60, you won't be able to go anywhere without seeing lingtrips, sometimes called the Queen of

Fruits. These intimidating-looking balls of fruit are covered in dozens of 30cm super-sharp spikes that protect a thick-layered pudding of jellied fruit. If you manage to get the spikes off without piercing yourself and you can break open the husk, then your reward is the jellied jusp centre, known to cure most ailments with the word ache at the end, particularly heartache, beard ache, toothache, tummy ache and arm ache. Jusp does not work for some words ending in ache, though, such as moustache, gouache, and panache.

It's worth remembering that lingtrips have been banned in public places in some craters because of their smell. When opened, a ripe lingtrip smells like a mouldy tennis sock that has been left to sweat in a bag for ten years with only flies for company.

An Earth rumour that we'd like to rein in is that moon people eat horses. We can assure you we don't, so please take that idea with a pinch of salt! We eat *with* horses a lot, though. They make excellent dining companions because they are full of tales and like us, they enjoy their mains. They tend to champ a lot and we tend to chomp a lot.

Another Earth rumour is that we like eating fat. This is also wide of the mark. We like chewing the fat, though, especially with wild horses, as they really know their onions when it comes to puddings.

Moon people like to eat their words, especially words with repeated letters, as they are more nutritious. Our favourites are taramasalata, knick-knack, senselessness, Woolloomooloo, and razzamatazz. Many of these fine words are popular with buttered parsnips. Tasty words like scrumptious, succulent, and delectable also go down a treat.

Some words you have to be careful of, because you can choke on them and they are difficult to spell. Words like ukulele, fluorescent, psychologist, onomatopoeia, rambunctious, obstreperous and narcissistic. Government is another one that can trouble you if you aren't fond of the letter n.

Then there are words that are hard to pronounce such as deterioration, specifically, and nuclear. These can lead to throat glot. A good drink of room temperature wishwater normally does the trick although words with lots of y and g letters are hard to shift, because they can hook around your clunk in between your tonsil cushions. Ziggy-zaggy is one word to avoid unless you have lots of cream with it. Giggling is another to chop up first before throwing down the foodpipe.

When it comes to drinking we enjoy a good slurp and glug. We drink water like you, but we can last longer than a camel rat without it, sometimes for as long as six months. Do you know what a camel rat is? Imagine a rat with two humps, long legs, a bad attitude and breath that stinks like a drain. That's a camel rat.

We store water in our heads for when we need it. This explains why we are never dehydrated and why our heads are swimming in thoughts and ideas. Water is drunk by every creature on the moon except horses, who refuse to drink it. They prefer brain nectar and diet jelly instead.

Moon people tend to drink enormous quantities of spilt milk from moon cows. These hilarious six-legged creatures have a reputation for being ham-fisted and are always falling over. The milk that they produce is called spilt milk and is all frothy like a cappuccino and has a very sweet taste. This isn't to be confused with cow water, which is something different.

A very popular drink on the moon is rock splosh. This amazing pick-me-up can be found in the centre of a rock and to get at it, you have to smash the rock to pieces. The traditional way of doing this, with lump hammers, takes time; so most people now just use a laser.

Inside the inner core of the rock is a delicate ball protected by dry ice. The ball itself isn't rock but a soft spongy orb covered in skin containing the splosh. The orb is placed over a bowl and punctured with a needle and the Splosh sploshes out. The skin then dissolves in this golden liquid once punctured and then it's ready to drink.

The health benefits of drinking rock splosh include better hearing after dark and the ability to smell sound. Remember that moon rocks are only ready for drinking when you see tears rolling down the side of one of its faces. If a rock isn't crying, then the splosh inside isn't ready, and you'd be wasting your time trying to get at it.

Other favourite moon drinks are the tears of clownfish, bog-cloud juice, black lemonade, kipper smoke, liquid ankle wax, mushroom pus, diesel, soda fluff and ferret flux.

We don't just drink liquids on the moon. We tend to drink a lot of gases, too, including larvae-lava gas, minch gas, pickle gas and fazz gas. We especially like drinking hinklepix. This makes our thoughts stand on end. They tickle us senseless and make us laugh like a drain being squeezed very tightly. Laughing at ourselves and others is what we do best on the moon. You might find it hard to believe that we can also drink the splishes of radio waves and the splashes of microwaves. Join us sometime!

MUSIC

Moon people love to boogie. They like music from all over the seven solar systems of the eastern quarter of the Milky Way, especially Wow-wow, Jim-Jam, Ping Ping, Mushroom, Boshmunga, Crunk, Green-Eyed Soul, Palm Beat, Bungee Mars Bass, Lumonics, Ragshoe and Turbo-Goat.

Musical chairs are everywhere on the moon, and you are bound to sit on a quite a few during your visit. All chairs on the moon are musical, whether they have legs or not. They learn music by picking up vibrations from whoever sits on them. When someone gets up and leaves, then they start to play the music of whoever has just vacated.

This is how many people pick an empty seat on a train. They listen out for the type of music being played, and if they like it, then they will sit on it. The chair then goes quiet and learns the vibes from its new occupant and waits for them to leave.

If you want to know what vibes you are giving off, then stand up and listen to your musical chair. You might like what you hear, but then again, you might not. Swapping to another chair might help if you don't like the music being played, but generally all chairs will play music by picking up on the sort of mood you are in.

On the moon, trees are planted with great thought and care. We look at the parts of the moon that get wind and those that don't. Trees tend to get planted in windy areas, because when the wind blows through them the music they make is awesome.

You will notice that many trees have holes up and down their trunks. These have been drilled by tree doctors, who know exactly where to drill without hurting a tree. The holes make the trees look like giant flutes. When the wind blows through these holes, tree music is made.

The sounds produced depend on the size of the holes, the type of tree and the strength of wind. When the wind blows through a wood or forest of trees that have holey trunks, the sounds made travel with real harmony.

Wood wind music is haunting, bewildering and captivating all at the same time. Oak trees with medium-sized holes in a gentle breeze will send your soul fluffy.

Many moon people love taking a walk through a moon wood, because they know their senses will be bombarded with musical greatness. Some trees don't produce the musical goods, though, and when that happens, we know that moon squirrels are up to no good.

Moon squirrels have an ultramarine body with a pure white tail, and they have a well-founded reputation for causing mischief. If a tree doesn't sound quite right, then that's because a moon squirrel and his mates have stuffed the holes with truffles or themselves and sometimes both. They do this to wind people up the wrong way.

They also do this because they like the thrill of being blown out of a hole when there is a sudden gust. They can fly out at such silly speeds, they endanger their lives. It's a good job their heads are made of steel. Truffles get splattered everywhere, which explains the splashes of brown splodge on tree trunks and their branches.

Have you ever wondered what music your mood would play if it could? Well, on the moon we have the technology to do just that, using music boxes. These amazing devices are about the size of a Martian cube mirror, and have the ability to read your feelings and turn them into music.

Music boxes are attached to sound walls in music shops. They don't sit on shelves – they are literally attached to the wall. Find one that you like the look of and pull it off. They come off quite easily, so don't pull too hard.

The music box will read your DNA and start mixing your data together to reflect the mood you are in. You might hear a few gurgling sounds and the music box might rock about a bit but that's normal.

After a few seconds, one of the box faces will eject a microchip. Take the microchip and place it in one of your ears. Your mood music will then play and download itself into your mindstream. Don't worry – the microchip is dissolvable. The music you hear is your music. If you don't like it, then you can change it by changing your mood and trying a music box again.

A music box will also download your mood music into a mouth wall to play in the shop randomly through the week, along with the mood music of other customers.

A mouth wall is a wall of skin covered in mouths that sing the music of music boxes. If your mood music is something other people like and it makes their soul twitch, they might ask for a microchip copy and the chance to meet you. When this happens, the music shop will write to you with the names and telephone numbers of people who are interested in your music.

If your mood music is something a music producer likes, then you could be invited to record some more at a cube studio.

Junk funk is by far the most popular musical genre on the moon. This is music made using recycled materials: furniture, gutters, fridge grates, metal bowls, petrol tanks, moon boards, barbed wire, gargoyles, cheese graters, gas pipes, shopping trolleys and kitchen sinks.

One junk funk instrument is the potwacka. This is made up of 30 pittypot and pattypot cooking lids, built on a frame of plumbing pipes hit with sticks and mallets. A potwacka produces a palette of sonic grooves ideal for jib dancing to.

Some people play bikelophones. These old and unwanted moon tandems have different sized holes drilled throughout their frames. The idea is that you take the seats off and blow into the frame covering the holes with your toes and fingers.

The sounds produced range from bliss trance to trance terror, depending on how hard you blow. It is an instrument made for two, although some clever moon folk can play two seats at once. The bikelophone uses so much breath that most players can only play for about ten seconds. Then they collapse.

Moon people have musical souls. Stand next to a moon person for long enough and you will hear their souls sing. We are always humming to ourselves, and everyone plays at least five instruments fluently.

From an early age, moon children learn to play NanoNino guitars, the smallest six-stringed guitars on the moon. They are small. Very small. In fact, they are about 10 mishymetres long, which is smaller than a piece of Gimble fluff.

These instruments produce a sound that can only be heard by baby moon dogs. We might not be able to hear the sounds but we can see them. You see, NanoNino guitars are played using brainwaves, and the sound vibrations produced are fed into bowls of liquid jollop. This makes patterns that are projected onto a large screen. Brainwaves are also used to play thumb pianos, circular harps and ring flutes.

Moon people love making vegetables into instruments. They make carrot flutes, turnip bongos, eggplant clappers, pepper trumpets, pumpkin drums and rhubarb violins.

It's always wise to use the freshest vegetables, as these make the freshest sounds and they can be used after playing to make a good wholesome soup. Vegetables that are a few weeks old make a rotten noise and taste like Hunduck breath.

One of the biggest vegetables on the moon is the bioballoon. This looks like a large intestine and grows on the surface of muck moss in moon meadows. These 200 ft giants inflate in sunlight and naturally breathe sounds through their skin.

When they inflate, they produce a vibrating sound, like a ruler being plucked on the side of a table. If it's an overcast sort of day, then they make a robust sound, which seems to be a cross between a tuba, the bassoon and a Saturn horn.

They don't need to be played, as such, because they naturally breathe their own sounds. If they are physically moved, then they give out a sound that is similar to the giggle of a snipblinker, which is a miniature hippopotamus, in case you haven't heard of one before. Vegetable instruments are normally played with elbows, toes, karate chops and noses.

Some of the most unusual music you will hear on the moon is produced by nature itself. On the shores of Zone 40, you will be drawn to sea steps where the ocean organs play. These are marble steps built on the quaysides that contain hundreds of musically tuned tubes, with whistle openings or air holes along the top row at pavement level.

As the sea hits the steps, musical chords are played as the steps breathe in air. New sounds are played as wave after wave hits the steps. No wave ever produces the same sound, and depending on the size of the wave, the music produced can range from tender to thunderous.

Moon people love to walk along the pavements and just listen to the music made by the waves. Some just like to sit in one place and breathe in whatever the waves produce. Sometimes the voices of our sea creatures can be heard as their sounds are picked up by the waves and are breathed in by the air holes to make music.

Zone 40 isn't everyone's idea of a holiday, though, because some moon people find it quite noisy. The sea never stops moving, so the music flows constantly. It's hard to find silence anywhere these days.

Moon people can play about 20,000 songs from memory. They have absolute pitch and can play any piece of music after hearing it once. They are able to detect and recognise not just one but multiple notes played at once with 100% precision and accuracy.

If a moon person sees someone else playing an instrument, don't be surprised to see them grab the instrument out of their hands and carry on playing. This is quite normal behaviour, and something moon concerts are famous for.

This means the audience and performers get a chance to swap places with each other, so that everyone is part of the whole experience. Earth people find it disconcerting at first to see the moon person sitting next to them get up out of their seat and push the piano player off his stool. After twenty minutes or so, Earth people are itching to have a go themselves, and some brave souls do.

Moon people believe that every number in the universe has its own unique sound. Earth people struggle to understand this, but you'll have to take our word for it. For example, the number 51 has an eerie and haunting sound, because it is lonely and spends most of its time on the perimeter of rectangles, looking in at all the other numbers playing.

The number 88,888 is one of the happiest numbers under the sun and sings up tempo vocal harmonies made up of nonsense syllables such as nick noop a cooka-looka, zippa-zippa dib-dab, dee dip da dee dip da zippa zippa do woo wah. They are happy-go-lucky sounds that make you want to click your fingers and clap your hands and tend to be used a lot by composers when writing music.

Seven is a violin full of tension, 34 sounds like a distressed waterbottle exploding, 100 sounds like a saxophone under arrest, and 144 is the sound of a deflating balloon.

So when moon people see numbers, they see music and hear it with their souls. Phone numbers are great fun on the moon, because each number produces its own sound. Combine those numbers and you get a unique ringtone.

One thing you will notice pretty quickly when moving about a moon city is that every street has its own music. Walk down one road and you'll hear perhaps some jiggy snizz. Turn left and it might be bishjollop. Turn right and it could be tigga. The music lives on the street in the same way the people do.

Where does it come from? Well, you might well ask. Look down. See the single green lines that hug the pavement? They have nothing to do with parking. They breathe music. The strange thing is that the music doesn't appear to come from the ground, but from the buildings above.

Earth people love just walking the streets on the moon, because they can't wait to find out what music is around the corner. We are asked whether the music drives us mad, because it is playing all the time. But we have never known anything different, and besides, it is turned off when it's time to rest.

Not all types of music can be heard on the moon. That's because some music is silent and can only be seen. Music that is seen but not heard appears to some people as a space, a colour, a pattern, a shape or a number. It can also be touched. We call the people that have this special "receivers".

For example, if ordinary moon people look through a keyhole, they will look to see what's on the other side. Receivers won't do that. They will look to see what's on the inside of a keyhole. That's because the space is home to silent music that only they can sense. Receivers say that keyhole space is made up of white, pink and blue music.

According to receivers, the sweet dreams of moon dogs are green number 2s covered in chickenpox and the souls of moon zebras are fractured purple rectangles that dance. To people who don't experience music like this, it might sound a bit odd. To people who do, it sounds a bit even.

The preservation of our environment is definitely on our list of Top Ten Things to Do. We are always thinking of new ways of keeping the moon green, and we are proud to be the winners of the Milky Way Green Cup again for the 12th decade in a row. Our ideas for upcycling and recycling have been copied and pasted in solar systems across our galaxy.

We began to think seriously green after some of the birds on the moon started to change colour and fall out of trees. The birds weren't able to fly again or sing. They just produced a load of foul language. No one at the time could explain why, but years later, we found out that it was the pollution from swear words hanging in the atmosphere. Everyone blamed everyone else for this, but the source of the swearing was eventually traced to a defective consonant machine that was run by arthritic vowels in an illegal word factory.

One thing you won't find on the moon is loo paper. It's a waste and it's not hurricane-proof. We dread to think how many trees have been flushed down the toilet over the years. To get to the bottom of this problem, moon scientists developed a new way of keeping clean. Here's what to do:

- After downloading, remain seated on the toilet. A silver flash in the pan then cleans your bottom using anti-muck technology, and after about three seconds, you are good to go.

- After visiting the toilet, you will need to wash your hands. On Earth, this involves water, hand towels or hand driers. On the moon it involves placing your hands inside a sink scanner which swipes and wipes your hands clean of all microbes using the same silver ion flash technology.

Like most places in the solar system we have a lot of poo. For years, all moon poo was collected, pointed at Earth and blasted into space, which then burned up as it passed through Earth's atmosphere. Earth astronomers used to think these were shooting stars, when in fact they were shooting poos coming to their natural end. It then dawned on us that poo was actually liquid gold. It could be used as a source of energy. Poo power is better for the environment, because it burns less carbon dioxide than fizzle fuels, fuzzle fuels and fazzle fuels. On average, the poo of 1,000 moon people will generate about 900 gugganuts, enough for 55 light orbs or 600 light rods.

When you see a half-moon from Earth, it's actually moon people doing their bit by turning off the lights. Sometimes we switch off more and sometimes less. One of our energy mottos is, 'Switch on to switching off'.

Most of us are pretty good at 'switching off', because light bulbs remind us all the time. They are the best energy monitors we have. Oh yes, we should mention that light bulbs on the moon speak, and some even shout if you don't pay attention to their energy saving wishes. If you try to leave a room without turning off the light, you will be told in no uncertain terms to do so.

If you pretend not to hear, then the light bulb will shout your name at the top of its voice and let the whole world know how lazy you are. You have no choice but to retrace your steps, which light bulbs hate, because this involves wasting even more energy.

Light bulbs prefer you to do a job right the first time, and most moon people do. Light bulbs don't negotiate; so don't try to argue with one, because you'll be fighting a losing battle. If you think using a dimmer switch will lower their volume, then think again – they aren't stupid.

A lot of people spend too much time talking, which releases a lot of hot air into the atmosphere and causes all sorts of problems for the Moon Air Authority. Moon people decided to cut down on chitchat and communicate more often telepathically. This does not mean that talk is out of bounds; it just means that moon people need to be vigilant and alert the authorities about excessive gasbags and jibber-jabbers who never know when to stop.

We are all encouraged to say what we want to say in as few words as possible. Some long-winded explanations have been known to blow people away; never to be seen again. Telepathy is a great alternative to mouth talking, because it cuts down on people getting their ears bent. This puts a strain on medical services, which in turn puts a strain on precious resources.

Look around the moon and what will you see a lot of? Footprints. They are everywhere and they are a menace. Footprints are a major threat to the moon landscape, as they can last for millions of years before disappearing.

Most people thought at one time this was because the moon had no erosion, wind or weather. Well, we have a lot of that. Footprints won't budge because they don't want to! They have a mind of their own.

The Moon Council for the Arts has ruled that footprints are a legitimate form of ground art and they should remain.

Some footprints have special protection and are listed as being of inter-spatial importance. Protected prints include Neil Armstrong and Buzz Aldrin from Earth and Stickney Tharsis from Mars. That's not to say you can roam anywhere and leave your mark. To prevent widespread footprint pollution, it is forbidden to walk in certain parts of the moon.

A problem far greater than abandoned footprints on the moon is single sock pollution. Odd socks seem to be everywhere, even though we can't see them. We can smell them, though, and there is a 100% chance you will too if you decide to visit the moon.

The Moon Office for Odd Socks (MOOS) receives many reported sightings of rogue socks across the moon and sends out special sock squads to deal with incidents as they happen. However, by the time the sock squads appear, the socks are long gone.

Theories about where socks disappear to vary. Sockologists at MOOS believe that some people on the moon literally work their socks off and they take off to get away from it all. Others argue that odd socks vanish when someone is told to pull their socks up. No one likes being told to improve their work or behaviour, so one or both sulky socks go AWOL.

Another theory is that paired socks often find themselves being mismatched, and so they go their separate ways to avoid a lifetime of misery. We think that they may hide inside desert crocker skulls or behind cloud drapes.

What is clear is that people never lose socks – the socks run away. Sock pollution is getting to be one of our most serious environmental problems on the moon because of the smells they pump into the atmosphere. Stale socks produce enormous amounts of toxins, and the longer they are missing, the worse the situation becomes. It is estimated that there are over eight million odd socks on the moon, and with only three recovered in the last year, we definitely have a problem on our hands.

All visitors to the moon are now required to register their socks with the Tourist Office for Even Socks (TOES) upon arrival. Anyone without an even number of socks will not be permitted entry to the moon.

Although we have a lot of respect for astronauts that have visited the moon, we are not happy with the clutter they have left behind. It seems as if the first astronauts here were more concerned about their moonprints than their carbon footprints.

Astronauts from Earth have been particularly untidy. Over the years, we have found all sorts of bits and pieces, including eye patches, golf balls, star maps, gold olive branches, oxygen tanks, slide rules, clothing, shopping trolleys, seismometers, photographs, flags, and car tyres.

Worse than that, astronauts have left behind home-grown bacteria. A lot of this bacteria has gone unnoticed, lying dormant for many years, but has since come to life and invaded organisms and habitats moonwide. The delicate moonmunks of Zone 21 were completely wiped out by a cold virus that could be traced back to Earth, and are now extinct.

It's not just Earth explorers we hold responsible. Astronauts from Mars and Uranus have been the worst offenders, leaving behind some of the worst music you have ever heard in the solar system. At least the music left behind by Earth astronauts was listenable. They have also left behind fractured spheres, asteroid cones, feathers, glass eyes and a bag of verrucas.

Many pieces of discarded exploration junk have been destroyed because of their contamination risk. Recently, moon scientists managed to stop bacteria from different worlds mixing to create mega-mugga viruses that could have wiped out all life on the moon.

One thing we don't like to waste on the moon is space. Wasting space is considered reckless, because some people don't have a lot of it, and if you have plenty, then it's only good manners to share it. If you do waste space, then you are known as a space cadet, which is like being told you are a waste of space. Wasting time is also a big no-no, because you could be busy saving the moon instead of biting your toenails.

The biggest waste on the moon is people not using their imaginations. Imagination waste is very serious, because it stops moon people from reaching their potential and it hinders moon progress.

Nothing is more powerful in space than the space in your own head, because that's where your imagination lives. If you don't wake it up, then your potential will always be asleep.

Moon authorities have realised the importance of helping people shake their imaginations into action, because there has been a 21% reduction in new inventions on the moon in the last 5 years.

To help combat this alarming trend, the Moon Institute for Creative Expression (MICE) has been set up to ensure that imaginations everywhere are up and about doing what they do best – prodding, provoking and mobilising brain cells.

You might see a lot of waste on the moon, but waste that has been given a new life. For example, there are over 50,000 bicycle punctures on the moon every year. The inner tubes aren't thrown away though. They make excellent belts and have become very fashionable. Some people even deliberately get a puncture just so they can wear an inner tube belt as a fashion accessory.

Many things on the moon have more than one function. Take jigsaws. In the past, most moon people bought a jigsaw, did the jigsaw and then stored the jigsaw away, only to get it out years later and wonder what to do with it, mostly because some pieces were missing.

Today, double-sided jigsaws have been made that are edible. The idea is to complete one jigsaw picture, take it apart and then reassemble it by turning all the pieces over to copy another picture. When both jigsaws have been completed, you can eat the individual pieces, as they are packed with nutrients called joggles, which are particularly good for helping fight off soul infections.

A 10,000-piece jigsaw can feed a family of four for about a week, although some moon people have been known to eat a whole jigsaw in one sitting.

WORK

Moon people have plenty of jobs to do on the moon. We actually never stop working, even when we are playing.

There are many unusual jobs to be done on the moon, such as prism shifting, quark cracking, diluting sonic booms, counting yeast cells, carving winds, scratching aprons, threading eyebrows, cleaning shock waves, and making sure that silent jars don't talk to each other. We have people to do all of these things.

We also have people that dissect blue giants, make idea hovercrafts, collect the static electricity from the dreams of stray kittens, rake ponds and tame wild funk-horses. It's the only place in the solar system where you will see space-pool skiffers and jegologists.

Some jobs are filthy, dangerous, and disgusting. Some are all of those things. For example, we have people who work as toenail chewers, footprint lickers, pong chasers, wuzzle buffers, and armpit dandruff harvesters.

One job that might turn your stomach is a fluff whiffer. Moon people are very good at recycling their belly button fluff, but not all fluff is suitable for salvaging, as some of it can stink. Fluff that has been left inside a belly button for a few weeks might not give off the most appealing aroma. A fluff whiffer will sort through thousands of balls of fluff, sniffing each one to see if they whiff or not. If they do, then they are fed to moon pigeons. They are surprisingly nutritious. If they don't, then balls of fluff might be used for pillows, duvets, cushions, cuddly toys, or slippers.

Next time you go to bed, think how many bits of fluff you are putting your head onto and who they might have come from.

Equally disgusting is the work performed by toe snufflers. These remarkable moon people have the unenviable job of smelling everyone's toes when they first enter a moonport and examing their feet for verrucae. This means they have to suck in the pong of sweaty and cheesy feet from across the solar system. Some feet have been travelling for months without ever having had a wash.

A toe snuffler will sniff each toe in turn to make sure they don't represent a threat to the delicate habitats of the moon and they will scan feet for feet warts.

No one is permitted to pass Gate 12 of the moonport if they have verrucae. If you do, then you are expected to make every effort to get rid of it within three days. If after that time, your feet are still covered in cauliflowers, then you are asked to leave.

Apostrophe agents are employed on the moon to spot and deal with the abuse of the apostrophe. The mistreatment of this punctuation mark is widespread, particularly in shops, signs and adverts, and they drive many moon people batty. Market stall holders seem to specialise in misplacing apostrophes, and apostrophe agents take great delight in issuing on the spot fines for careless use. If you see a sign saying *Rubber Banana's For Sale*, then you have a duty to report it.

Apostrophe agents will also spend a great deal of their time looking for missing apostrophes and letters. You can help. If you see a notice saying *Smile, Your on*

Camera, then call an apostrophe agent without delay to deal with the situation. Never try to sort out an apostrophe incident yourself, as it is a job for highly trained professionals.

Some moon people work as finders and the chances are you will use one whilst you're here. A finder is someone who will hunt for something you want or need, such as a hairy balloon, a rose frozen in liquid nitrogen or a box of jumbled ideas. Finders love their jobs because they get to explore the moon looking for the weird, the wonderful and the ordinary.

You might want a watering can filled with purple anger. A finder will find it. You might need a teaspoon of radiation fog. A finder will find it. Or what about a hat stand that whispers to jellyfish? A finder will find it. Some things might take longer to find than others, such as identical snowflakes, musical bananas or music that is 44 days old. Whatever it is you are after, a finder will find it eventually.

Finders have a 100% success rate, of which they are rightly proud. They'll be able to find you the light at the end of the tunnel, if that's what you are looking for. To find a finder yourself, ask at your hotel reception and they'll soon introduce you to one.

The only thing a finder won't be able to find for you is a job on the moon. Moon jobs are only performed by moon people. We know that this might be disappointing, because so many Earth tourists have told us how they would give their right arm to be a logic gatekeeper, a dinglewit designer or a flick coach.

Some people on the moon work as noise quashers. These highly skilled engineers spend their time getting rid of noises by matching sounds so they cancel each other out. When two sounds mix, together they can make silence, which is music to the ears of a moon quasher. Not all sounds mix together in this way, and sometimes a bigger noise can be made.

For example, if you combine the loud cracking warble of a griker bird with a wockle cough, then you get a real ear bashing. But if you mix together the woosh of a click with the wash of a clock, then you get absolute hush. And that's why we need noise quashers.

You see, sometimes we need some peace and quiet, but we can't always get it, especially if one of our neighbours has a nunk that yips all day. Noise quashers spend most of their time dealing with noisy neighbours by finding a sound that will neutralise their raucous pets. Sometimes they have to do this discreetly by hiding a creature in a tree.

So, if someone has a moon cat that snores all day in the back garden, then this will drive next door mad because their snores are louder than pneumatic drills. A moon quasher could help, though, because they might put a mooze bird in a tree. They make a sound like a waterfall and that cancels out a moon cat snore, and so your garden will be lovely and peaceful.

As you know, moon people are always losing their eyeballs, and so we have a team of moon people who go everywhere picking them up and cleaning them. Eye catchers are employed in every zone to clear the streets of eyeballs to avoid people stepping on them.

If an eye catcher is in the right place at the right time, then some eyeballs are caught even before they've had a chance to touch the ground. This is rare, but it does happen.

It's not a job for the squeamish, because a lot of the eyeballs found are in pretty bad shape. Some are covered in grit, many are bloodshot, some have been pecked at and quite a few have been squashed. Eye catchers will endeavour to return all missing eyeballs to their owners after a through clean and a period in quarantine.

Some moon people don't seem to do much at all. It looks like they are doing nothing, but they are actually quite busy working their socks off thinking something through. They tend to think of things that no one else would ever dream of, and we call them professional wonderers. These are not to be confused with professional wanderers, who spend most of their time tracking and smelling astronaut footprints across the moonscape.

Professional wonderers might ponder whether an insect trapped in amber can dream of seaweed. They might think about whether freeze-dried ideas are better for you than fresh ones. They might wonder how many inflatable numbers in Crater 67 have hairy insides.

None of these ponderings seem relevant to many people, but they often help us to find the answer to another question. For example, a cure for knee unhappiness was found after someone sitting next to a professional wonderer posed the question, 'Can clairvoyant shipwrecks taste dolphin shadows?'

One of the most demanding and tedious jobs on the moon is counting the grains of sand that go inside egg timers. Every grain has to be examined to make sure it will fit through an egg-timer hole, and each one is individually polished fifty times by hand before being used. Counting grains has to be precise, because egg timers are used for various cooking tasks that demand absolute accuracy.

A bludge egg boiled for one second more than it should can make all the difference between it being the most delicious egg you have ever tasted, or you being covered in exploding green yolk from head to toe.

Egg timers have to be accurate because they are used for measuring other important tasks such as the time taken for ideas to freeze or for paint to dry.

Story weavers have one of the best jobs on the moon. They move from zone to zone inside a train of thought, looking for discarded threads of stories, which they then knit together into a patchwork tale.

Story threads can be found pretty much anywhere. Some blow about in the wind, some dangle from trees, and some can be found under furniture.

Story threads consist of single or double yarns, and they come in many different colours, textures and materials.

Story weavers tend to work alone, but they have been known to join together if their ideas are threadbare. Once a story has been woven to a satisfactory standard, it is then shared with a circle of gabs, who wrap it around their minds and then give it a good shake. This releases a lot of story dust into the atmosphere, which is breathed in by anyone within a 20km radius.

Gabs will move around the moon shaking their minds in as many zones as they can before swallowing themselves and burping their souls into space.

Some people have jobs that don't seem to serve any particular purpose, but they obviously do, because the moon authorities tell us that they do. And that's all they say. They like to keep some jobs secret, and so we don't question too much because we know we won't get an answer.

Some jobs that we have no idea about include people who scream into holes in the ground, people who throw whispers into caves, people who taste ear wax and people who hide behind trees.

You might also see people bending light, chasing wrinkles, babysitting clocks, dusting gravity, whistling up trees, itching arrows or kicking buckets.

Ask anyone doing any of these jobs and they will probably just smile at you and say they are too busy to talk.

HEALTH

Moon people are blessed with excellent health and can live for about 300 years. That might sound like a long time to you, but it's a blink of a jidnapper's eye in the history of the universe. We have a saying on the moon: 'Enjoy your ice cream before it melts', which is why we are always on the go enjoying our ice cream.

Our immune systems were developed by copying and pasting the DNA of Earth crocodiles, mosquitoes and old tjikko trees and mixing them all together, so we are a pretty tough bunch. We do get sick, though, and that tends to be our own fault. Most illnesses are not life threatening, just major inconveniences to our busy and interesting lives.

The most common health problem we see on the moon is people choking on words. As you know, moon people love words, but they can sometimes cause problems. Last year, 13 people died of adjective obstruction.

Some people are addicted to words and they literally can't stop using them. This always ends up being quite messy, with word addicts suffering from logorrhoea. This is a bit like mouth diarrhoea and it's not very pleasant to be around when it happens. If you can, try to avoid word-lovers and wordsmiths, because they are the moon people most likely to suffer from this problem.

When someone starts to dribble puns or spoonerisms, then it's time to take cover. Within seconds, hundreds of long words are ejected from the vocabularian's mouth at great speed, leaving you little chance to duck. You are covered in a niffy wet spaghetti-like matter called 'gob-spludge'. Not only is this hugely embarrassing but the pong can last for days and no amount of fragrance can get rid of it!

Verbal vomiters all vow never to flaunt their word prowess again, but they just cannot stay true to their word, and so gob-spludge time after time. This explains why the hospitals are always busy.

Our top scientists, the headcases, are developing a new device called a 'word choker', which may solve the problem. It's a collar worn around the neck that can detect a build-up of waffle in the voice box. Before the waffle is allowed to enter the mouth, the collar warms up and convoluted words are irradiated.

Word chokers have been successfully trialled on a sample of moon manglers: obnoxious animals that swear and burp all the time. The chokers have eradicated their foul language and stopped them from polluting our atmosphere; a problem we've had for decades. The side effects of using a word choker include pirouetting, smelly feet, underarm consonant sweating and speaking in a very low voice. In some instances, moon manglers have grown Mohicans and developed rusty freckles. Clearly, there is still a lot of work to do before the word choker is deemed safe, but it will be worth the wait.

Quite a lot of our visits to sick bays are related to accidents or phobias. Moon people have a lot of phobias, although not as many as Earth people.

Phobias make us do silly things that often result in mishaps and sometimes tishpaps, which are like mishaps but ten times worse. One phobia people really get worked up about is the fear of gravity reversing itself. Moon folks suffering from this believe that one day they will fall upwards and crash into a magnetic ceiling. They tend to stay indoors a lot and they avoid large open spaces if they do venture outside. As a result, they get sick of being inside.

Another unusual fear that some are jinxed with is the fear of the letters i and j being next to each other. This is why you will never see them doing a jigsaw, doing a jive with a 'thingamajig' or anyone called Jimmy, saying "I'll see you in a jiffy", or jingling their loose change. The idea of doing ju-jitsu in their jim-jams just gives them the jitters.

If you think these phobias are bad, then what about those people that are afraid of being chased by Siamese peacocks, or being sucked down a plughole, or of balloons popping?

Then there is the fear of odd numbers. People with this phobia always tune the televisions onto an even numbered channel and have the volume to an even number as well. They do things twice in order to avoid doing something an odd number of times. Reading a book is a waste of time, because they can only read the even numbered pages, so a story never makes any sense. They can only have friends who have phone numbers that are odd. This makes all their friends a bit odd, too.

There is a sickness on the moon called the dizzles. This is related to the moon's unique and peculiar rotations. In the first two months of the year, before 12 p.m., the Northern Hemisphere of the moon rotates in a clockwise direction, but after 12 p.m., it rotates anti-clockwise. The opposite happens in the Southern hemisphere. This can reverse time and speed it up, which plays havoc with plant growth in some moon craters and people have complained that they don't know whether they are coming or going.

You will soon know if you have the dizzles as it involves walking, talking and thinking backwards amongst many other things. 'Dizzlers', as we call anyone with the dizzles, find it hard to cope with the sudden change of rotation and everything they do ends up going the other way. They are simply unable to tell their bodies that everything is fine and that the moon is still the moon, despite it spinning the other way.

Earth people have described the dizzles as a cocktail mix of tobogganing, zorbing, looping the loop and bungee jumping all rolled into one. Earth people who have suffered a bad case of the dizzles go home with such utter mind mash that they often tell their friends stories about the moon which simply aren't true. This leads to all manner of tall stories and confusing tales; so it's no wonder people have funny ideas about moon life.

Most Earth people will bust a gut to get to the moon because of the health benefits. You will find a number of new health clubs across the moon called 'Shedders', and they are proving extremely popular with overweight Earth visitors. These massive health clubs guarantee that anyone visiting from Earth will lose weight as soon as they step through the door. Wait (weight) a minute, though. Does that sound too good to be true? Would you be wasting (waisting) your time?

You are right to be suspicious, although the health club isn't strictly telling you a lie – they are just not telling you the whole story of life here on the moon. You see the moon's gravitational pull is one-sixth that of the Earth.

For example, let's imagine that your Dad weighs 60 bags of cement on Earth. Well, on the moon, he would weigh just 10 bags of cement instantly. As soon as he came back down to Earth, he would weigh 60 bags again. Don't be fooled by the solar system travel agents who sell weight loss holidays to the moon. You will lose weight, but only whilst you are there! If you want to lose weight, then the best thing to do is to exercise regularly and cut down on those moonpies!

Mind splinters are something we get a lot of on the moon. When we have something on our mind, we tend to chop up our thoughts into pieces, which can lead to splinters, and these can pierce our ideas and make them bleed.

Mind splinters are dangerous because they are full of germs, and so our minds can get infected unless quickly treated. This can lead to people talking out of character and making fools of themselves with words that have become swollen and septic. Some moon people can't always tell if they have a splinter lodged in their minds, because they become infected over time.

An untreated mind splinter can lead to broken dreams, fractured feelings and a niggling feeling at the back of the mind. Anyone with a mind splinter complains that they can't cast their mind back, they have mind flashes, they are often in two minds, and they can't mind their own business. They also notice that their mind's eye can get a bit blurry, they can't make up their mind, their mind goes blank and they sometimes lose their mind.

Multiple mind splinters are extremely dangerous because they can lead to mind slips and eventual mind rot. Anyone with a mind splinter is normally referred to a specialist, who can remove them with the latest in 'mind over matter' mental tweezers. The splinters are literally talked out of a patient's head through careful negotiation. Recovery is a slow process, because ideas have to be stitched up and this can leave mental scarring that lasts years.

A serious health problem on the moon is laughing too much. Moon people laugh a lot, but sometimes this can get out of hand and cause prickly laughs and giggle fitting. This condition is no laughing matter, as anyone who has suffered with it will tell you.

Giggle fits can start off innocently enough after some harmless leg pulling, or seeing a moon puffer explode, but they soon pick up speed if encouraged. A giggle fit can lead to laughing up your sleeve, laughing like a drain or laughing all the way to the bank. The most serious giggle fits begin with a belly laugh and end with laughing your head off. That's messy and no one finds it funny. To die laughing is more common here than you might imagine.

Giggle fitting is treated by making people laugh on the other side of their faces. This involves being laughed out of court and laughed off stage. Having a laugh is important whilst you are on the moon, but try not to get carried away or the chances are – you will be!

101 THINGS NOT TO TRUST

There are some things on the moon you just shouldn't trust. For example, you should never trust flying carpets of cheese with mice on them. They have a hidden agenda. You should also be wary of hole-less sponges, distressed combs, accurate horoscopes, countless numbers and common sense. Watch out for blonks. They have anger management issues and eat batteries.

There are many more things we feel obliged to draw your attention to, so your visit is not spoilt. Our advice is to be aware and always trust your instincts. If you are unsure or you don't understand then ask a moonraker, who will help you overstand until you are as clear as mud.

1. Moon combs. They have teeth and they are not afraid of using them.
2. Bitter lemons. They are hostile and rude. So are bitter winds.
3. Plastic surgeons. They take years to biodegrade. Always choose a real surgeon.
4. Talking wallpaper. Some of it is evil.
5. Tourist traps. They are worse than mousetraps.
6. People who say they are on Cloud 9. They aren't. They are probably on Cloud 7 or 8.
7. Moon pegs. You don't know what a pinch is until you've been pinched by a moon peg.
8. Garden paths. You don't know where they lead.

9. Clocks. If you are having a great time, then you don't need to know the time.

10. Moon people who say that tomorrow's yesterday is today's future. They are normally from ghost triangles.

11. Glass balloons. They are full of sand and are lethal when they pop.

12. Butterflies that only eat margarine.

13. Moon pollen. Get a bit of this up your snout and you'll sneeze yourself home.

14. Moon snakes … because they swallow themselves and then explode.

15. Tables that walk in pairs. They mean business.

16. Odd and ends. Always trust evens and starts instead.

17. Craters that hum as you approach them.

18. Retired telescopes.

19. Balls that roll up hills.

20. Moonbows that have holes in them.

21. Full stops without a sentence.

22. Shadows that don't change size.

23. Apples without pips.

24. Moon people that wear their hearts on their sleeves. Very messy.

25. Pumpkins that taste of chicken. The pumpkin probably ate one.

26. Moon people with two left hands.

27. Dentists. They are all trained on Mars.

28. White moon cats after dark. They vomit three-pronged nish noodles.

29. Yellow snow.

30. Things you can catch but can't throw.

31. Words that contain x, y and z.

32. Infrared cabbages.
33. People that steal your thunder.
34. Moon flowers that whistle or burp.
35. Moon crosswords – the clues never add up.
36. Gasbags. You don't know where they have been.
37. Polluted gravity fields. Stand too close and you'll get pulled in.
38. Door-to-door earwax salesmen.
39. Pineapples that don't pine.
40. People that offer you the Earth, but have no soil.
41. Non-stop flights to the Northern Ceiling. How will you get off?
42. Space cracks. They are often full of space spiders.
43. Trips offered to Pluto. It's closed.
44. Miniature ostrich eggs that float above candles. They will get on your wick after a while.
45. Trumpets made of Vaseline. Blow one and you'll find out why.
46. Body furniture, especially tongue and cheek chairs.
47. Moon slugs that ask for directions to Crater 6. They are elite pickpockets.
48. People who say that they have been 'here, there and everywhere'. They have probably been nowhere.
49. Words that do not rhyme with purple.
50. Moon people who can lick their own elbows.
51. Burps that come from mini-craters.
52. Intelligent carpets. They can tell if you are wearing slippers or not.
53. Grains of sand. They're on the run.
54. Self-licking stamps.
55. Moon eggs with less than six yolks. They are probably off.

56. People full of beans. They are normally full of wind.
57. Self-stacking cards. They can also self-destruct.
58. Moon shadows. They have hidden depths.
59. Horseflies. They are vicious and hide in square bubbles.
60. Shapes with seven sides that say they are octagons. They're not.
61. Reversible parachutes. They might be fashionable, but they aren't safe.
62. Knisper birds, knasper chicks or knusper feathers.
63. Moon lard. It tends to stink and will follow you around the house if you leave it unwrapped.
64. Out of date barcodes. They don't know what they are doing.
65. Speaking plugholes. They get into arguments with water.
66. Valentine cards sent from Venus. They are full of mush and acid.
67. Moon people who say they have a thousand voices.
68. Road toads. They are poisonous, two-faced and lie through their back teeth. Don't be afraid to answer one back.
69. Red dolphins. They sell faulty brain cells.
70. Fake rain. It is so shallow.
71. A pim-pam-pum. It can pack a punch that will send you into next week and back.
72. Nesting dolls. Once released, they can run faster than a cric, and they are almost impossible to catch.
73. Magic bees. Their honey is not what it seems.
74. Hummingbirds that know the words. They refuse to hum.
75. Remote controlled chopsticks. They could go anywhere.

76. Skids. They remember everything, but say nothing.
77. Frozen think tanks. They were frozen for a reason.
78. The shade. It thinks it is cooler than the rest of us and we have no time for show-offs.
79. Moonquakes that last for longer than five minutes. Those that do are up to something.
80. Cakes longer than 3m. They are full of sog-nush in the middle.
81. Flying carrots that hide inside air pouches.
82. Space spiders. They crawl through space undetected and their webs are lethal.
83. Moon turtles. They never tell the truth about their age, and they never let on what they keep inside their shells.
84. Puddles that move as you approach them. They always change direction at the last second.
85. Tunnels of wind, tunnels of fire and tunnels of midge-natchers.
86. The fruit of sarcasm and hard-boiled problems.
87. Anyone that says they work in the Hair Force. This no longer exists since the moon cutbacks in 129.
88. Circus artists. They can't draw and their paintings are awful.
89. Skipping moon tigers. They have no rhythm.
90. Trees running low on magnetism. They tend to get depressed.
91. Green-coated crisps. They have sweated for too long.
92. A flish flash, a fish flash or a flush flash.
93. Alarm clocks made by moon magpies. They are full of toenails.
94. Traffic lights. They have seven colours and some swap places with each other.

95. Trampolines. These are for decorative purposes only on the moon, and they do not bounce.
96. Earmuffs. They are very scratchy and they will bring your ears out in a rash.
97. A bolt from the blue. A bolt from the yellow is far more reliable.
98. Moon opticians. They are all unqualified and many can't see the wood for the trees.
99. A restaurant that asks you for your order in Morse code.
100. Hard-boiled hats. They stain your head blue and they speak too quickly.
101. Owls stuffed with missing jigsaw pieces. They talk in riddles and their words have jagged edges.

CRYING

Moon people cry all the time. We like it. Crying helps to clear the tubes and tunnels of our minds, and we enjoy the feeling of tears as they travel down our cheeks. They tickle.

Tears come in different flavours, too, and so it's always nice to taste something new. Do you know that moon people cry in different accents and colours as well? You will soon learn to spot the difference between cries from the Northern Hemisphere and cries from the Southern Hemisphere.

A Northern cry has a rising tone and a Southern cry has a falling melody. Equator tears tend to warble in between. Some people will cry pink tears, some blue and some yellow.

People in the Tip Tops don't cry that much because it's too hot there, and tears dry up pretty quickly if they do. This leaves tear stains on their faces that look like freckles.

Moon people like to cry with others, so don't be surprised if you get invited to someone's house for a cry party. If you do cry by yourself on the moon, then it is customary to do this with a hologram copy of yourself.

One thing you mustn't do on the moon is cry into or onto a mirror, because this frightens tears and worries mirrors. Tears aren't used to seeing their reflections and mirrors feel threatened.

When a moon person cries, their neck glands fill with water and they empty into a flap of skin under the chin called a chin satchel. Tears are sucked away from here by tubes that connect directly to eye corners when a good cry is imminent.

We cry from all of our eyes, including our mind's eye, so we can get fairly wet if we are having a good blub. When we cry, the tears might flow thick and fast, or they might take their time. It depends what we cry about.

We might cry because we can hear our cheeks chatting to each other, and they always talk nonsense. They think we can't hear them, so we have to laugh without them knowing. Silent tears of laughter stream down our faces when they natter away to each other.

We might cry with laughter because we see someone fall over who then tries to pretend they haven't. That is always a laugh.

Tears might roll if we see a woffa bird. These are birds with no sense of direction that tend to fly into windows a lot. They seem to think that they can fly through glass like slinky birds, but they can't, and they never seem to get the message. Some moon people think that woffa birds do know that they can't fly through a closed window, but they do it because they like the attention.

We might be moved to tears by listening to lost voices. Moon people are always losing their voices and it takes ages to find them again. Sometimes they are never found.

When moon people cry, they produce enough tears to fill a kettle. In fact, many moon people actually use kettles to catch their tears in. They then put the kettle on, and when the tears have boiled, the steam produced enters the atmosphere as a cloud.

Now, if the tears cried were unhappy ones, then the cloud releases raindrops of misery on someone else, which is completely unfair. You could get lucky, though, and get rained on by a happy cloud produced by the kettle of someone who cried tears of laughter into it.

If moon people cry for more than two minutes without a kettle, then a puddle is inevitable. This puddle is licked up by moon dogs, who then inherit the soul of the moon person who has just blubbed. Moon dogs then adopt the characteristics and behaviour of the tear shredder concerned.

This explains why moon dogs have multiple personality disorders, because on average, they lick 200 puddles a year. We have a saying,

'It's wise never to trust a moon dog. You don't know who it's been'.

Moon dogs cry, too, which is scary when you think about it. They produce their own puddles, and moon dogs love licking up each other's puddles. This explains why they are so mixed up.

One thing we do a lot of on the moon is cry over spilled milk. We do this because milk tends to be quite salty and the sweetness of our tears tends to calm it down a bit.

Whenever we have a glass of milk, we place the glass on a table and fill it right to the very top. This makes it ridiculously hard to drink without spilling. It is especially hard because straws were banned on the moon after the 'Last Straw' incident of 2001.

To get around the problem, we deliberately kick the table legs, which spill quite a lot of milk everywhere. Next, we look at a picture of a sad puppy, which makes us cry, and we aim our tears over the spilled milk. We then lick the milk off the table. To leave any just isn't on, so always make sure that every last drop spilled is licked from sight. Be careful of splinters, though.

You might be wondering why we don't just pick up a glass and spill the milk. That's because picking up a full glass of milk contravenes at least three laws on the moon. You might also be wondering why we don't just pour the milk over the table and forget all about the glass. That's because table manners are everything, and this would just be plain rude.

Don't be too alarmed if someone in the street runs alongside you and starts crying on your shoulder. This is normal. The easiest thing to do if this happens is to just go with the flow.

Moon people cry on other people's shoulders because crying is messy and we don't like messing up our own clothes. Crying normally involves quite a bit of snot, and so smearing it on someone else's shoulder saves messing up a perfectly clean handkerchief. This explains why you will see many people with soggy shoulders and slimy snail trials.

It's considered polite to leave a wet shoulder to dry by itself, so don't be tempted to wipe anything away or change your top. If you fancy crying on someone's shoulder yourself then make sure you can reach. There's nothing worse than misjudging someone's height and crying into their elbow instead. This isn't popular, so choose carefully.

You will see a lot of people in tears on the moon. Try not to be too concerned if you see people crying when out and about, especially going into banks.

Anyone that cries going into a bank is normally in floods of tears and laughing at the same time. This is because banks are funny places and tend to operate like joke shops.

You might hear people actually describe their bank as a joke. People that say this usually cry on their way out of a bank, too, because they are reduced to tears. Some don't know whether to laugh or cry, so they do both.

You may have worked out by now that moon people don't really cry tears of unhappiness. Any type of unhappy crying was officially banned in 1999 because people got sick of it and we ran out of kettles. This means that sobbing, wailing, weeping, bawling and snivelling are strictly forbidden. Crocodile tears were not included in the ban, so they are fine, as long as they are used sparingly.

Around this time, it was advised that moon people avoid situations conducive to crying, such as chopping transparent live onions, reading poems from the edge of space, or pulling out nose hairs.

Other situations the Eye Council recommend sidestepping are shoes made of biscuits, dictionary picnics, stale pogo sticks and talking with door-to-door pompoms trying to sell you dreams. All these things will end in tears, and not ones that will be easy to wipe away.

Moon people enjoy making other people cry. They do this because they like to make others laugh. Happy crying is positively encouraged, because it's good for the heart, and tears of happiness are bottled and sold to Earth to cheer people up.

Tears of happiness are so popular on Earth that we struggle to keep up with demand. We've now got hundreds of people employed to cry all day. Their feet are covered in salt and licked by goats. This is extremely ticklish and produces floods of laughter. Even the goats laugh. We've also employed thousands of town criers to make people laugh in the streets.

Some countries on Earth are debating whether to put tears of happiness into the water supply. What is there to discuss? Folks on Neptune have been doing this for centuries, and look how happy they are. Their whole world is at peace now after 700 years of war and devastation. Honestly, Earth people can be their own worst enemies sometimes. No wonder they are light years behind. It's a crying shame.

So crying is now big business on the moon and we are doing pretty well out of it. Our sales figures are out of this world compared to last year, and we've just started exporting to other solar systems. Planets that we've never heard of are showing quite a bit of interest, which tells us that there must be quite a bit of misery out there.

It's probably not right that we should be looking to find fed-up planets to profit from, but we are helping to remove glumness, despair, and in lots of cases, gloom and doom.

Exporting laughter to improve our bit of the universe gives everyone the feel-good factor. It is our goal to have every solar system laughing at themselves and crying their eyes out by the end of 4030. As long as we can keep the tears of happiness flowing, then I'm sure we will all be richer for it. Morally richer, that is.

Moon people love crying their hearts out. This normally happens when they are watching a funny film. They get to a state where they just laugh and cry uncontrollably and lots of tiny red tattooed hearts appear all over their skin.

They appear to almost stop breathing as tears roll down their face, and then, out of nowhere, they burst into an enormous laugh. This releases the tattooed hearts from the skin surface and they flutter into the air, crashing into each other and popping into a red mist. This amazing event is hilarious and often makes people watching cry their hearts out, too. Some lose their eyes too and things start to get silly.

Crying has been proven to seriously improve people's health. Scientists at the Eye Told You So Institute say that crying for at least 68 minutes a day helps improve your foresight by reducing mind wax clogging, and it also helps clean your soul of impurities.

They say that all moon people should learn how to cry properly. A proper cry can give you a whole body workout, which in turn helps you to feel great.

A study of 28,072 moon people and found that 98.9% felt better after a good cry. Researchers discovered that regular criers reported being able to run further, climb stairs twice as fast and find better places to hide when playing hide and seek.

People that didn't cry as much were found to be clumsier and unable to laugh when unpeeling a banana. Scientists are working with health centres to set up crying workshops around the moon to help teach people how to cry and get the most out of their tears. They believe that crying before bedtime is the best time to cry because it gives your mind a good wash.

People aren't the only ones that cry on the moon. Flat tyres, failed experiments, dripping taps, broken buttons, snapped laces, cracked windows and untitled books all cry. They all have good reasons for crying, just like stubbed toes, trapped fingers, exhausted elbows and crackly knees.

Other things don't seem to have an obvious reason for crying. These include magnets, wigs, gas masks, dandruff, zigzags, handkerchiefs, and numbers. They all cry about something, but what, we don't know.

In fact, we think that there are thousands of things that cry on the moon, but we can't always tell, because they cry when we aren't really looking. For years, we didn't realise that telephones and teeth cried, until they were placed on a round-the-clock watch and washed in ultra-violet light.

We hadn't even thought about fish crying until quite recently, but they get choked up about all sorts of things, particularly seaweed fights and burping dolphins. This explains why the moon's oceans and seas rise dramatically and why we are trying to get fish to cry less.

Sleep

You are probably wondering how moon people sleep. Well, all moon people sleep standing up, with one face eye open and one face eye closed. The eye that is open is asleep and the shut-eye is awake. Back eyes cannot close, so they remain open. Moon people are remarkably similar to Earth dolphins, because when they fancy forty winks, two brains shut down whilst the other stays alert. They do this because they don't trust anyone, so they prefer to keep an eye on things, just in case anyone pulls faces at them.

Most moon people like to sleep in short bursts (six minutes for men, seven minutes for women and 30 for children), rather than in one long stretch.

Speaking of stretches, be careful not to stand too close to a sleeping moon person, because 10 seconds before they wake up, they erupt into a vigorous stretching routine called the fundingle. This involves various quick-fire karate chops, three deep burps, two warbling whistles and an expulsion of choking green gas from the rear end. Not pleasant, I'm sure you'll agree.

Oddly, the fundingle has been copied by tourists and is now a dance craze on Earth and is beginning to catch on in Mars. All moon people find this insulting.

Most moon people will sleep burst three times a day when they feel tired, rather than at a set time in the day. Although moon people can go without sleep for a week, this is considered to be dangerous to the environment.

This is because their fundingle routine goes haywire and gets confused. On occasions, this can be quite explosive.

Insomnia is unheard of on the moon, because people don't know how to spell it. For this reason, it was banned in 1996. In fact, any word that is tricky to spell or explain has been expelled from moon talk. Don't bother looking for the following words in a moon dictionary, because you won't find them: accommodation, queue, comb, electricity and receive. Thousands of other words are now extinct, so be careful what you say when you visit, or you'll really put your foot in it and you'll be sent home.

Moon people are known throughout the Milky Way for their machine gun-like snorty laughs and these always erupt 30 seconds before a sleep burst.

It's worth knowing that you will never see a moon person yawning. Not only is yawning considered very rude on the moon, it is also dangerous, because it uses up valuable air supplies. If everyone on the moon was to yawn at the same time, then all the oxygen would disappear and the whole moon race would evaporate and shower Earth in laughing ladybirds.

But wait, what's this about oxygen? You were probably told on Earth that the moon doesn't have any atmosphere. Well, we do, and quite a lot of it, as well, but we kept it a secret until recently.

You see, when humans first invaded the moon on 20th July, 1969, we could see them coming, so we all hid in the lunar highlands. There's plenty of room there, and we all took a deep breath before the oxygen was sucked out of the atmosphere and stored in the oxytainer, a gargantuan tank buried deep inside the moon's core.

The humans that landed didn't stay long anyway. They danced around a bit, said something about mankind or a man being kind, and planted a flag, which fell down 5 minutes after they took off in their rickety space rocket. Apparently, the flag was turned into a pair of curtains by a reclusive couple living in the moon mountains.

Moon people love to dream. In fact, they are the solar system's most prolific dreamers. You might think your dreams are weird, but the sleeping thoughts of a moon person are in a league of their own. We know an incredible amount about the dreamlands of moon people, because we can see them.

You can probably remember that we sleep with one eye open and the other closed. You will also recall that the open eye is really asleep and the closed one is awake. Well, the open eye acts as a data projector and is able to beam a dream onto a surface like a wall as a moving picture. Unfortunately, there is no sound, but the actual picture quality is stunning. It's like watching TV or being at the cinema.

Most moon people are very careful where they stand when sleeping and will make sure their open eye doesn't face a big building or fence.

Dreams are very private things. However, lots of moon people simply aren't bothered if anyone sees their dreams and some purposely make sure they face a wall, so everyone can see what they are dreaming. On Earth, this is called attention-seeking and on the moon, this is called ego-gravitating.

Sometimes the dreams that are broadcast attract no attention whatsoever, but other dreams can draw quite a crowd and cause a bit of a scene. They then end up being repeated and broadcast as films on TV. One famous dream is that of Clementine Fizzler, a moon elder from just outside the Volcanic Ring. You are bound to hear about her dream whilst you are here.

Apparently, Clementine took her normal Tuesday morning trip into Meltdown Meadows Shopping Pod to stock up on jib-jabs, flembools and kapper pipes when she suddenly felt all the life in her body grind to a halt. She knew what was going to happen, but could do nothing about it.

A tsunami of tiredness washed over Clementine and she just stopped in her tracks and started to sleep. Where? She stopped right outside The Gloo-Glux Department Store, the biggest shop on the moon – the shop with a white wall bigger than a blue whale.

But it wasn't the wall that Clementine's dream was beamed onto. No, she was facing the other way. A small man with a big, bald head was sitting on a rest pod eating his lunch, and Clementine's dream was being broadcast right on the back of his head!

Clementine's dream was more than a bit peculiar, even by moon standards. It showed thousands of tiny grand pianos falling from the sky in a frightening but spectacular downpour; each piano the size of a raindrop. As each piano drop splashed onto the ground, it filled the air with music and then exploded into zillions of miniature zebras, each one wearing ice skates and ridden by green starfish.

Within moments of beaming her dream, Clementine, without knowing, had sucked passers-by into her world like a vacuum cleaner consuming space dust. At first, it was the buoyant classical music that seemed to turn heads. Not only was it hypnotically soothing and gentle, it made everyone levitate 10cm off the ground. It really was uplifting. Imagine seeing a load of people all floating above the ground, smiling at the back of a bald man's head. Peculiar, especially as the man was not aware of what was going on around him.

After two minutes, Clementine's dream went into a slow motion sequence, which was even more transfixing. As the pianos were falling, they were actually folding inside out, revealing inside kaleidoscopic notes waltzing with numbers.

You could also see words moon walking, with dictionaries and wishbones doing the can-can. This couldn't be seen in normal dream motion. At the moment of impact when the piano drops hit the ground, the slow motion sequence showed each keyboard opening, releasing 88 red, yellow, blue and red balloons floating into space, which then popped into musical heaven.

The pianos themselves then dissolved and transformed into zebras, like nothing you have ever seen in your life. Their eyes and tongues were chequered like chessboards, they had ice skates instead of hooves, and their stripes travelled horizontally across their bodies. The starfish that rode them were angry-looking and blew red bubbles.

You can imagine what a sight this must have been for the 100-strong crowd that had now gathered in awe to watch what happened next. In fact, this was causing so much of a scene that the moon police had to close off the road and cordon off the area. No one else was allowed to watch. This was a rare event. The last time a road was closed off because of a dream was in the summer of 2090.

You might be wondering why the police didn't just wake Clementine and end it there and then, but there is one thing you should never do to a moon person, and that is wake them from a dream. It's not the law; just something that everyone obeys, because we know that it can be very hazardous to do so. We wouldn't dream of waking you from one of your dreams, either.

Occasionally, a moon person is awakened by an over-eager tourist, and this always ends in tears. You see, to stir a moon person from a dream is a bit like poking a silverback gorilla with a stick. Don't expect a smile and a big hug. The moon person unlucky enough to be woken up gives out a yelp the size of Jupiter and then quite literally explodes.

As you know, moon people's insides are a strange mixture of blue cheese, honey, mushy peas, and a slimy, glowing yellow mucus, which temporarily paralyses anything it touches. Pieces go everywhere, and the mess is unbelievable. A thorough clean-up operation might take anything up to a year to complete. A particularly bad explosion might mean it is easier to replace everything rather than attempt to clean it.

The worst part of a broken dream not only means everyone gets covered in goo and mushy peas, but all those watching suffer from a broken heart. This isn't surprising, really, because it is very distressing to see a moon person just blow up.

You might be wondering what happens to a dream if someone is woken up. Well, the dream freezes and the image it is showing at the moment of disturbance is tattooed onto the surface it is being beamed onto. This explains some of the surreal murals you'll sometimes see on the side of walls and on the back of some bald heads.

Fortunately, no one disturbed Clementine from her dream. Her projection lasted for 11 minutes and 50 seconds, and then she burst into her fundingle routine and the dream simply floated into space and disappeared from sight.

All dreams do this and glide through a universe until they reach Dreamland, a sort of solar system twice the size of ours. There are no planets there, just gargantuan spinning dream diaries that suck their favourite dreams into their pages.

The dream diaries are colossal, and contain all the dreams anyone has ever had on the moon or on Earth since time began. They also contain every dream had by every animal. People dream that one day they will be able to visit Dreamland itself, but people really good at maths have worked out that it would take nine billion years to get there and six days to find the centre.

Our dreams are always projected as a round picture and measure about 50cm across. This can be made bigger by touching the circle a desired number of times, although it is considered very rude to touch another person's dream without their permission. To get their agreement you have to do this before they fall asleep.

If you are lucky, you might see a handful of dreams on one wall. This amazing spectacle can be mesmerising for moon tourists, as well as for moon people themselves. If you're very lucky, you might see some dream circles overlap, a bit like a Venn diagram. If this happens then the dreams mix together and the creative jumble is truly jaw-dropping.

In fact, many tourists walk round with their mouths open for hours at a time because of the many amazing things they see on the moon. Earth people are especially prone to jaw-dropping moments, which is why they swallow so many moon flies. This also explains why they choke a lot, too, although not always straightaway. A moon fly will sit in someone's stomach for at least an hour before getting bored and then trying to fly out.

We have a saying on the moon that morning dreams come true. For this to happen, a morning dream has to take place between the first cuckle crow and the sound of daybreak.

If you have never heard daybreak, it is like a cloud cracking up after hearing a really good joke. We used to think that the saying was just a load of hogwash, but it isn't. Dreams really do come true during this time. Talk to anyone about a morning dream and they will be only too glad to tell you.

Sharing the content of your dreams is always a fun thing to do when you have had one, even if the details are a bit sketchy. Moon people will love trying to interpret what is going on in your head. Some think they are experts at explaining dreams. Don't take too much notice, though, as only you know what the dreams mean and other people are only guessing.

Some people say that dreaming of a swimming baboon with bad breath wearing bagels as armbands signifies that you don't like doing your homework.

Some might say that playing hoopla at a fair with your own halo whilst keeping a hiccup hostage suggests you like sticking your nose into other people's business.

Dreaming of ventriloquist maggots in a tub of angry margarine performing magic tricks signifies that you are a bit weird.

A dream about kilt-wearing kangaroos performing karaoke to kingfishers could mean you like eating furry strawberries with sour cream.

If you are serious about getting your dreams interpreted, then visiting one of our many supermarkets is recommended. This is where you will find a dream counter and a pleasant waiting area.

Take a dream ticket with a printed number from the desk and then wait until your number is called. When your number is up, whisper your dream into a seashell and then hand it to one of the dream crackers behind the counter. They will then listen to your dream and interpret it for you using the latest eye-closing technology. The dream is decoded and you are given its meaning on a scrappy bit of paper written in red crayon.

Dream crackers do not discuss their interpretations and they offer a no refund service, so if you think they are talking rubbish then you are probably right.

The supermarket will even sell your dreams, with permission. You can buy someone else's dream – with the interpretation to match – as a projection to take home with you.

The Top 10 'In Your Dreams' at the time of writing are as follows:

1. If you dream of a blue rabbit chasing you with no ears, toothache and a ginger accent, this indicates you need a holiday.
2. If you dream of an accordion playing cards with conkers, this suggests you are ready to try your first acupuncture session.
3. If you dream of an alarm clock floating above a candle inside a circle of crocodiles with albino eyes, this suggests you are worried about the health of your fingers.
4. If you see a zookeeper and a jealous teddy bear playing table tennis with violins, this means you probably don't like losing.

5. If you dream of an abusive ladybird painting a rungless ladder next to a tablecloth, this suggests you are in the wrong job.

6. If you dream of a one-eyed giraffe standing on an iceberg eating a glove with a glow-stick round its neck, this indicates that you are afraid of commitment.

7. If you dream about cuckoos, the Morse code and dirty nappies, this probably means you like the smell of darkness.

8. If you dream of a Christmas cracker being pulled by two cream crackers then you know what this means already.

9. If you dream you are doing a crossword in the middle of a crossroads whilst wearing a pirate's hat and an eye-patch, this signifies you have eaten too many caterpillars.

10. If you dream the sky is full of cat's eyes and you feel like you need the toilet, this indicates that you are afraid of your dentist.

Sport

Moon people and Earth people share one main thing in common: a love of sport. However, sport on the moon is quite different to the sport found on Earth.

Exercising Caution

Moon people like to exercise, and they particularly like to exercise caution. We like this form of exercise because we have to watch our step, and it is something we can do without having to go to the gym. We don't have to wear special clothes, either, so it saves on the washing. It's also something we do every day, because living on the moon demands you exercise caution at all times – we never know what's around the corner from one minute to the next!

The amount of caution you have to exercise obviously depends on what you are doing, and some activities use more calories than you might imagine. Crossing the road can be dangerous, so this burns a lot of mental calories. It can also burn a lot of physical ones if the road you are crossing is 1km wide and you have to dodge moon blips, as they tend to drive with one eye open and one eye closed.

You certainly have to exercise caution when naming your children, because you might give them a name that others will poke fun at, so research is essential. You might think calling your baby girl Bobbles is very sweet, but dig into the origin of the name and you'll find it actually means 'face sweat'. No one wants to be called that, but according to our moon records, there are at least 308 children called this living in the Northern Hemisphere and 190 in the Southern Hemisphere. Some people say that exercising caution is the only exercise you need to do, because if you do it every day, then it keeps you fit and ready for anything.

Orb Lift

Visit a park on the moon and you will almost certainly see moon people playing orb lift. Two players sit in front of a board of 25 squares each, containing an egg cup holding coloured orbs the size of tennis balls. Each row contains alternate red and blue orbs, except the middle square, which has a white orb. Players choose either red or blue as their colour. The idea of the game is for players to meditate and lift each of their orbs out of the egg cups, so they float above them using mind over matter. This incredible mind game is something moon people have played for generations, and demands a great deal of mind control.

The game begins when the referee hits a triangle three times. Players then focus on the orb they want to lift and try to lift all twelve of their orbs before their opponent. Players don't take it in turns, but meditate at the same time, trying to mentally lift all of their orbs before the other.

When the winning twelfth orb is lifted, the middle white orb lifts itself automatically, and all the opponent's orbs fall back into their cups. The twelve winning orbs then spin in the air and the game is over.

Players are permitted to lower their opponent's orbs if they want, so the game can get quite tactical. Spectators who have the power to mind lift are not allowed to interfere in a game. This happened in the Orb Lift Championships one year and caused chaos. Master orbists have been known to play with boards containing 64 squares.

Cloud Herding

Cloud Herding is an amazing sport to see whilst you are on the Moon and the Wing Crater is the place to see it. The aim of Cloud Herding is for Cloud Shepherds to move a squadron of sheep-shaped clouds into a hole in the sky using Aeropenguins. These are robotic flying penguins with wind in their veins able to perform remarkable aerial manoeuvres at the command of their shepherd owners. They have the brain of a dolphin and the heart of a cheetah so they are clever and strong in equal measure.

Competitors stand on the tallest mountain in the Wing Crater and take turns to launch their Aeropenguin into the sky to guide a collection of roaming clouds into a unique hole in the sky called the Sky Cave.

A Sky Shepherd will whistle commands to an Aeropenguin and one by one the clouds are rounded up and edged into the Sky Cave. Whistle commands tend to be unique to each shepherd and their Aeropenguin. Each competitor is timed and the Aeropenguin who can herd all the clouds in the quickest time wins.

Aeropenguins and shepherds have their work cut out with some clouds which can be stubborn and temperamental. Sometimes an Aeropenguin will be erratic too or fail to hear a command and clouds spread all over the place making a shepherd's job a tough one. Clouds that are successfully steered into a Sky Cave are blown out after an hour for the next competitor to try.

Some Cloud Herding competitions demand that clouds are driven around the tips of other mountains to make things more challenging. Other competitions use threatening weather to try and put off Aeropenguins. The clouds used in these competitions are the shape of a clenched fist and they will chase an Aeropenguin if it shows any fear.

Towel Throwing

Throwing in the towel has become a popular sport amongst moon people in recent years. This involves throwing a towel into a linen basket from a distance of 15m. Competitors are able to choose their own towels, but they cannot be any smaller than a tea towel. Any material is permitted.

The game is simple enough, but it is made more challenging by getting competitors to make and wear a towel animal on their heads, which has to stay in place during a match. This is a towel shaped into an animal shape. Making swans are popular. They also have to wear a towel sling on one arm, which makes throwing much harder.

Some games require throwers to wear a towel round the waist, too. To make towel throwing even more challenging, throwers can be 'towel whipped' by a maximum of three rivals in an attempt to sabotage a throw. The first person to throw a towel into a linen basket without it touching the sides is declared the winner.

Losing competitors are then blindfolded with their towels and made to find their way home without peeking. Some even have a flannel placed in their mouth, so they can't ask for directions.

Déjà vu Football

Déjà vu football is an intriguing game to watch and play. It is played in a similar way to football on Earth, except our teams have two goalkeepers per team, because the goals are bigger. We also play with a musical ball and a game is played for 120 minutes. The rules are the same, except that when the final whistle is blown, the ball explodes. The whole game is then played again without a ball. This means that players need incredible memories, because every pass, every kick and every goal has to be replayed exactly as it was in the first game.

Crowds love watching the same game twice, even if the second time round they know the score and there is no ball. People will say that they have seen a good match if the first game matched the second game. If a team wins away from home, then they get to select any player from the opposing team who has to clean their boots.

Jigga-Juggling

Jigga-juggling is a great favourite with many moon people. This involves jigging and juggling at the same time. This sport started on Neptune, but we have adapted it and made it moon-friendly. The rules for jigga-juggling are simple: competitors must juggle seven objects whilst jiggling over agreed distances. If an object is dropped, then the jigga-juggler must return to the start. Jigglers jog for 20 steps, then hop, then shake their bottoms and turn around.

Objects used for jigga-juggling can be anything under the sun. A popular choice is to use wedgenoggers. These are like Earth hedgehogs, but with spikes that can give you mild electric shocks. Gloves are not permitted. Only moon adults are allowed to jigga-juggle with wedgenoggers because they tend to spit quite a lot as they are thrown into the air. If you drop a wedgenogger when jigga-juggling, be prepared to have your shins kicked. They hate being dropped and they will soon let you know how unhappy they are.

Other objects used for jigga-juggling include moon pipes, bashjappers (hamster-like creatures that shout 'Weeeee' when thrown in the air), balls of jelly, stinging bricks, and echo cushions. The annual Jigga-Juggling Moon Championships include races between 100 metres to 50km and two-legged relay races.

Telekinetic Basketball

Telekinetic basketball is also very popular on the moon. This is like Earth basketball but without physically touching the ball. Players bounce the ball, pass it between team members and shoot baskets using the power of the mind. This might be hard to get your head around, but moon people are pretty good at using their minds to move objects.

Players place one hand over the basketball and literally ask it to bounce or move to another player. With practice, and plenty of it, players can dribble, finger spin and perform all sorts of fancy tricks just by mind- talking to the ball. Seeing a catch for the first time will probably blow your mind, because the ball isn't really caught, it is stopped before it hits the hand and hovers.

The best players can alter the course of a ball in mid-flight just by asking it to. This requires considerable skill and thousands of hours of practice. Dribbling is probably the hardest skill to master, and many young players practising for the first time tend to dribble from the mouth rather than dribble with the ball.

Moon Marathons

When you look at the sports section of moon newspapers, you can't fail to notice reports about moon marathons. These are competitions where moon people pit their stamina against that of a posse of jixi-jibbles. These are two-headed red sheep with attitude problems that only breathe through the nose.

The course is 100km long, with many unusual challenges and obstacles to overcome along the way. The ridiculously slippy slopes are a great test of endurance, and the moon deserts are no picnic. The ultimate aim is to complete the course and beat the first pair of jixi-jibbles to the finish line.

Jixi-Jibbles are notorious for cheating, which makes this sport particularly entertaining, but they seldom get away with it. Moon people are given a 35-minute head start before about 20 jixi-jibbles are released. These creatures can appear quite intimidating when they set off together because they squeal like peacocks being tickled and let off an enormous amount of steam from their knees when they pick up speed. They also release a lot of bottom-generated gas when they get excited. Moon athletes train all year for moon marathons and are highly respected for their commitment and lunacy.

Tennis

If you're looking for something a little less physically strenuous, you'd be better off playing tennis. We have two versions. Two-handed tennis is played with a racket in each hand and follows the same rules as Martian tennis, using four balls on a round court. Another game of tennis we play is word tennis. Players hit words to each other by using the end letter of one word as the starting letter of a new word. For example, if one player says 'Echo', then the next word has to begin with the letter 'o', such as Octopus. Rallies can last for seconds or hours, depending on the word power and concentration levels of players.

Some competitions have a word limit. If players reach this limit, then both players are challenged to write a story using all the words exchanged. Rules vary, but some competitions actually make it a rule that these words have to be used in a story in the order they appeared when playing word tennis.

A typical word rally might go something like this: traffic, codswallop, punchbag, ground, doppelganger, reverse, Egyptian, nostril, leech, hysteria, acapella, acupuncture, eyeball, labyrinth, hopscotch, herbivore, elf, flimflam, masquerade, escape. Try it for yourseves!

Other sports

There have been some sports that have come and gone over the years. Punty wobbling was popular in the fifth decade before moon independence, but then fizzled out after new sunlight laws were passed. Feddle pipping and splat quacking were other victims of this era, too.

Some sports have banned altogether, including piff wixing, snoot drubbing, and clack sunking. The sports of whip snaffling and click fibbing have also disappeared. These sports were deemed too dangerous after various accidents and some unfortunate crowd incidents.

There are many sports still around and we recommend that you give some of them a go before your time with us comes to an end. Don't just watch; take part – you'll only regret it otherwise when you're on the moon shuttle going home.

Laughing

Laughing is the thing we most like to do on the moon. Everyone laughs, and it's contagious. When you arrive on the moon, and we've had a good laugh at your passport photograph, we give you some nitrous oxide to breathe in for 20 seconds. Don't worry, this won't hurt you, it's just laughing gas. We like to get you chortling the moment you've arrived.

You can probably guess why working at a shuttle port is a popular job with moon people, and why the waiting list for a position as a customs officer is 50 years.

Every day starts with a laugh when you are on the moon. First thing in the morning, moon people will look in the mirror, take one look at their hair and burst out laughing. I think you do the same on Earth, too.

After a quick shower, it's over to the local park, where people meet for a group laugh. This is a great way to begin the day. Laughter leaders get everyone doing a few mouth stretches and then a giggle warm-up, which involves keeping the eyes wide open and belting out loud, ape-like shrieks. This is followed by a group hokee-cokee and a conga around the park.

We laugh a lot because it has been proven that laughter is healthy for you, but we know that overdoing it isn't a good idea.

We don't bother with gyms on the moon. Our top joyologists found that laughing 100 times a day is the equivalent of swimming butterfly for 6km. Most people laugh more than this, although laughing too much means you don't always get your jobs done. Inner laughing is called for when laughing out loud is inappropriate.

The best types of laughs to have are the belly blasts. These start off with people scrunching up their eyes and bouncing their shoulders up and down. Laughter at this stage is soundless. The belly laugher then starts to cry and the eyes start to open. Then it happens. A deep, hearty laugh explodes from the depths and this produces trails of uncontrollable snot and ear wax, thigh slapping, and breathlessness.

Occasionally, the belly laugher comes up for air, only to fall about pleading for it to stop whilst smacking the ground. Anyone having a belly blast laugh might look like they are in pain, but they are actually in a land of happiness and don't really want it to end. Belly laughs are even better than seeing someone fall over into a puddle of moon dog vomit.

Collecting

Moon people like collecting toenails. They press them into cream crackers covered with butter and display them in magnetic cabinets.

They also like collecting fish dreams. To do this, they go fishing in moon lakes. To catch a moon fish, you stare into the water, whistle and then wait for one to come to the surface. When it does, you stare at each other and smile. The trick is to hypnotise a fish so that it will release its thoughts and fantasies.

A sure sign that a fish is mesmerised is when its eyeballs change colour and rotate. This is when dream transfers take place. Dreams are passed into our eyes as invisible data streams and splash into our brains, where they find somewhere to swim.

To release a fish dream from your mind, you lie in an empty bath and stare at the ceiling, where the dream is projected from your eyes. Oddly, fish dreams don't feature water or sharks. Their dreams tend to involve cartwheeling, remote controlled green snow, angel wings, straws, hairspray, the number 5.25 and silk shoelaces.

Moon people who collect fish dreams often paint the dreams they see and sell them to aquariums. Moon people also collect the dreams of elephants, lampposts, black mirrors, organic acrobats and tired calculators.

Moon people like collecting and carving eggshells. The shells come from a wide variety of animals across the moon and they make sensational pieces of art.

The gump bird lays eggs that are perfect for egg carving. These giant birds are twice the size of emus and look almost the same; except they have pink and green feathers and their hearing and eyesight aren't as good. Some wear glasses.

Their glossy eggs are enormous and almost three times the size of an Earth emu egg. They are rounder in shape and they can be any colour.

Moon people used to race gump birds in the past, but this stopped after it was obvious they had no sense of direction. What makes the eggs of gump birds unusual is that they don't contain a yolk. They don't appear to contain anything but they are stuffed with gump dreams. Every egg has a different coloured inner shell, and some have been known to have a furry inside, but these are rare.

Egg artists will shape intricate patterns into these remarkable eggs using a laser and create faces, planets, animals, and lattices. Some collectors even turn them into lampshades.

Moon people are very careful about the eggs they collect, as some are protected and cannot be touched. The eggs from thinker birds contain ideas in embryo that have to be allowed to hatch naturally.

Forcing an idea out of an egg before it is ready is reckless because the idea might be a life-saving one, or it could be a new invention with potential to transform the solar system forever.

Nose Picking

Nose picking is an enormously favourite thing to do on the moon and you will often see moon people using their big toes to perform the act. This involves putting your leg behind your head and positioning the foot in such a way that the toe has easy access to the left or right nasal passages.

Sometimes people excavate their nose tunnels with their little toes, as these can extend when required to reach all the hard to get to places. Moon people are quite supple and contortionism tends to be something in our bones.

Nose picking with fingers was banned after the last Moon Olympics and it's something we don't really talk about now. We'd appreciate it if you didn't, either.

Moon people actually collect the contents of their snouts, which I am sure you will find revolting. We use mini-rolling pins to flatten our nasal nasties and make collages out of them.

You will often see snot collages in the big hotels and offices across the moon, as they brighten up foyers and corridors. Snot collages of celebrities and famous people are displayed in modern art museums and are popular with moon people and tourists alike.

Boo Buk

One hobby moon people love playing is boo buk, which is a soundless quarrelling game. It involves quite a bit of staring and basically turns into a 'no blinking' competition, which we understand people like to play on Earth. For moon people without eyelids, the rules are changed to 'the first person to need the toilet'.

Contestants decide what it is they would like to argue about and then they sit opposite each other and start squabbling using only their eyes. Obviously speaking is not permitted and the only rule is the 'Sounds aloud are not allowed' rule. A sound is defined as, 'any nugget of noise that fractures silence into a thousand pieces.'

So if you produce a snuffle, a sniffle, a groan, a grumble, a grunt, a chuckle, a cough, a snizzle, a sneeze or an actual word, then you are out. Pulling funny faces is permitted and this tactic is normally the one that provokes a sound explosion of some sort in your opponent. The winner is then allowed to boogie on the spot and wiggle their bottom for 30 seconds.

In cities across the moon, you will see boo buk bays. These are shops where you can go in and challenge a complete stranger to a game if you have nothing much else to do, or enter a competition.

The game of boo buk is strangely addictive and has been known to take over some people's lives. In fact, some moon people spend all day playing. By the way, no one from Earth has ever beaten a citizen of the moon, so if you want to make a name for yourself and you fancy your chances, then find the nearest boo buk bay and give it a whirl!

Mischief

Moon people love practical jokes and are known throughout the solar system for their enjoyment of mischief. One thing some of us like to do is plant random objects in random places, so that people are always kept on their toes and on the lookout for the unusual. Finding something in a place where it doesn't belong can be really quite thought-provoking and very satisfying.

You might be taking a stroll through the open moonscapes of Crater Wishless when you see before you a field filled with hundreds and hundreds of poles. Not that unusual, perhaps, but on top of the poles stand plastic cows with red antlers on their heads. They all face south except one, which faces north and has blue antlers. Why are they there and who put them there?

The problem with being a first-time tourist is that you never know whether what you are looking at is in place or out of place. You could be shopping and you notice that all the pumpkins have Mexican moustaches. Is that normal? Yes, for the moon it is. Pumpkins here look like that.

You could be at one of our many fantastic swimming pools and you notice that underwater there are glass jars filled with miniature trumpets stuck to the floor. Is this normal? Yes, they like it there.

Then again, you could be at a library and you can't fail to notice that the floor is covered in red rice. Is this normal? Is it normal to see trees in the street with oxygen masks strapped to their trunks? Is it normal to find slices of toast stuck to the ceiling of your hotel bedroom? Do all street corners have hat stands wrapped in gold blankets? Whether the objects you see around you are there by mistake, by design or by mischief, we don't interfere.

Fence Jibbing

Fence jibbing is a craze that's swept the moon in recent years. This involves finding a stretch of fence along a field or roadside and jibbing something into it.

This started off with someone jibbing a pair of glasses into a fence bordering Crater Q. Gradually, over a period of months, the fence had been jibbed over a thousand times, with people adding their own glasses to the fence. A sight for sore eyes, according to some people but this fence is now a tourist attraction, with fresh jibbings every day!

Fence jibbers never know if the item they leave will lead a lonely existence or be joined by an army of others. There are some fences that have just one or two things tied to them and they stay that way for years. Then there are fences that are full from top to bottom, end to end.

People have added moon dog shoelaces, string fingers, wishing collars, dream ropes, one-legged trousers, curly toenails, cat scarves, pipes, sellotape balls, apples hung from ribbons and gish tails.

Fence jibbing isn't actually allowed, but the moon authorities tolerate it. The trick to pulling off a successful jib is to do it when no one is around and look innocent. Most moon people never look like they are up to mischief, so it's hard to spot anyone doing anything out of the ordinary.

Earth people always get caught because of the guilty looks they give out. They stand out a mile and besides, they don't move quickly enough. Most moon people can execute a jib in a jiffy, which is about 1/16th of a second.

Guerilla Gardening

Another hobby moon people like to participate in when no one is looking is guerrilla gardening. This involves climbing into someone's garden when they are out and planting some quirky seeds, barmy bulbs or potty plants without them knowing. This gives you the chance to kickstart an empty garden to life or to give an established garden an unusual twist.

The most popular seeds to secretly plant are hulking solar blossoms. These are like Earth sunflowers. They grow to about 20m and have 1m-wide heads that burst with pink, blue, yellow and green. Guerrilla gardeners from different craters try to outwit each other by secretly visiting each other's gardens to see who can plant the most seeds.

Guerrilla gardening is becoming so popular now that people have started to plant in neglected public spaces like the Moon Quad, Zig Square in Crater 2 and the Gishna Centre next to the moonport. The best guerrilla gardeners find cracks in walls and pavements, so that our streets are more colourful, fragrant and edible.

Guerrilla gardening is closely related to feng shui hijack, but this is only permitted between friends and family.

Feng Shui Hijack

Feng shui hijack involves moving the furniture and objects in someone's home and rearranging them in the most ridiculous way possible. Moon people do this all the time, whether someone is at home or not.

If someone is at home, then feng shui hijacking isn't easy but it is possible. For example, when visiting the toilet, hijackers take the opportunity to rearrange a bedroom or when someone leaves the room to make a drink, they make the most of the time alone to move and hide things.

If you have a spare key to someone's house, then you can spend hours moving furniture from one room to another, so that things are a real mess for when your friend or relation gets home. This might explain why a moon person's home never looks quite right.

Although feng shui hijack can be annoying, we find it highly amusing and always get our own back anyway.

If you have time, try to find out more about some of the other things moon people like to do, such as whistling in moon caves, throwing boomerangs at rainbows, or wock picking. You might also like to find out about horse skiing, talking to sky holes, hole hovering, wish stroking and dressing up as a moon penguin.

FESTIVALS

Moon people celebrate a wide spectrum of festivals that are fun and offbeat. There is a festival for pretty much everything on the moon, and they come in all shapes and sizes.

The Red Spot Festival

Many festivals are devoted to the other planets, moons and moonlets of the solar system. The Red Spot Festival is held every April for six days, in honour of Jupiter's Great Red Spot. This is when Jupiter is the clearest in the sky. Moon people believe the spot is actually a bloodshot eye that watches over the Earth and moon without ever sleeping.

People paint their faces red, dress in orange clothes and spin anticlockwise for up to 10 hours until they faint. Be aware, though, that Jupiter's gravity is stronger during the festival, which causes some people to lose their heads, literally, so it might not be suitable for children.

Not to be left out, some moon people gather to celebrate Saturn's rings. They believe that the rings spend a certain number of years around a chosen planet before hopping to another planet. One day they will leave Saturn and orbit the Earth.

The Ringed Jewel Festival is a romantic event held in February and this is the time when many people propose to a loved one. The rings are symbols of everlasting love. Many moon people don't celebrate this festival because they see it as a bit sloppy and slushy. The festival is a great place to learn more about Venn diagrams, though, and there are workshops for learning how to hula-hoop, too.

Music Festivals

Music festivals take place on the moon throughout one cycle of the sun. They are normally held in deep craters so the noise doesn't disturb anyone. The biggest music festival on the moon is Buzz. This hugely successful event features the very best in solar system music with a mad mix of styles including space-noiz, sky, solar dub, solar wind and all manner of great music from rising stars and binary stars.

Previous years at Buzz have featured Techno Coconuts and the Gravity Timelords, Space Cactus, White Dwarf and the Gas Giants, Sonic Silence, Plastic Universe, Andromeda Migraine and Parallax.

Buzz has a reputation for being the place where mega-groups are born and two of the most famous played their first gig here: Echo Reflections and The Flawed Senses.

In addition to the music, you will find solar theatre, space poetry, lunar gardens, levitation circles, cosmic comedy, wish workshops, upside down trampolining, moon mayhem art, pulsar performances, and food from the inner planets. Buzz takes place every year from 1-13 June in the organic Continuum Crater, Zone 78.

The Moon Film Festival

The Moon Film Festival is an event that most moon people look forward to. The latest feature films, documentaries and animations from across the moon and throughout the solar system are showcased for all to enjoy.

Watching a film on the moon is a bit different to watching a film on Earth. Films are beamed onto huge screens of white material in the sky called flix-bibs. You might be wondering how flix-bibs stay in the sky. Well, that's a job for the moon bod birds. Four moon bods are needed for a flix-bib screen, one on each corner. They fly 150m into the sky, stretch the flix-bib screen with their talons and flap like mad to stay in one place so the screen doesn't move.

The film is then beamed onto the flix-bib for people to watch. Sound is transmitted through the open mouths of moon bods. The sound quality is excellent except if a moon bod has a sore throat or a cough.

Films have different category ratings, so that people know whether a film makes suitable viewing or not. There are two ratings: G and R. If a film has a G rating, it means it is Great. If it has an R rating, it means its Rubbish. Surprisingly, more people enjoy watching R-rated films than G-rated films. The film festival takes place every September at venues across the Moon.

The Day of the Moonraker Festival

Early each November, moon people pack a hamper and head for the D Crater to celebrate the Day of the Moonraker. This wacky festival is a firm favourite with people in the Northern Hemisphere, although all are welcome. All you need is a rake.

The Day of the Moonraker plays tribute to some wise folks from a village in Middle Earth who outwitted their local authorities. The Moonrakers were making illegal booze or moonshine and the tax men had plans to stop them by paying them a surprise visit. The raid took place at night, but the local people had a tip-off that it was to take place. They disposed of the illegal bottles of whiskey in the village pond. It was a still, moonlit night when the customs men raided the village, and the bottles could be seen at the bottom of the pond. The locals fetched rakes and pretended to be stupid by trying to rake the reflection of the moon off the surface of the pond in order to disturb the surface so that the customs men could not see what was hidden at the bottom.

Moon people love to re-enact this tale by raking ponds of water, pretending they can see the moon or some cheese that has rolled in. Children normally dress up as the Moonrakers and the adults pretend to be the tax collectors.

The Big Fat Fib Festival

Every third Saturday in August since 1010, moon people have gathered in Crater MM to celebrate the Big Fat Fib Festival. Contestants take the stage in front of a huge crowd and they get three minutes to spin the most incredible tall tale they can think of whilst keeping a straight face.

A team of expert liars from Mars award points for exaggeration, humour, stage presence and storytelling ability. The winner is awarded with the Baron Munchhausen Trophy and the title of The Biggest Fibber on the Moon. This is a whopper of a trophy and measures over 33m high.

The festival is held in a beautiful part of the moon, with lots of garden paths to explore. People will try and lead you up these and encourage you to plant some seeds of suspicion. You do have to be extra cautious visiting the festival, though, because it's the one place on the moon where you will be taken for a ride, even though there are no rides to go on.

There are workshops in spinning yarn, stretching the truth and leg-pulling. Everyone is welcome, except people who do not have back teeth, as they will not be able to lie without them. If you enjoy being economical with the truth, then the Big Fat Fib Festival is not to be missed.

The Micro-Festival

The Micro-Festival is a popular little festival that takes place every year inside a small puddle just outside the Moon Belt Crater. This festival is for microorganisms only.

The Micro-Festival celebrates all things small and is the place to sample micro-cooking, see micro-wind turbines, ride micro-waves, tour the latest micro-houses, play hide and seek with parasites and boogie with friendly bacteria. The Micro-Festival is by invitation only.

The Mind Warp Festival

The Mind Warp Festival bills itself as the festival of all festivals, and many would agree. Mind Warp is relatively new to the moon and if you haven't seen it before then it's likely to blow your mind. Moon people who have seen it before still can't believe their eyes. In fact, after a Mind Warp Festival, the biggest mess to clean up is eyeballs that have popped out. Quite a lot get squashed, which isn't pleasant.

Mind Warp involves contestants throwing objects such as bags of flour, melons, and coconuts as far as they can, using only their minds. Some can reach distances as far as 200m. Other competitors try to stop their opponents from throwing by using their minds to try and cause mid-air explosions, which can be hilarious. The event can get messy and all spectators are required to wear safety goggles and helmets, as some of the debris can be dangerous.

For some strange reason, moon people like to throw things and other throwing festivals take place through the year, but using arms instead of minds.

The Mooning Festival

The Mooning Festival is an event that most moon people pretend doesn't take place. Some would say that it has a bare-faced cheek to describe itself as a festival at all.

There is a moon monorail that runs from the Northern Ceiling to the Southern Floor and it passes through many zones along its way. One zone it travels through is Zone 2-Twenty-2, which is where hundreds of moon miffles gather on both sides of the track for about 12 miles. Moon miffles are mischievous creatures that live off broken alphabets and practise practical jokes on each other. When a train passes, the moon miffles give everyone a wave and then they turn around, bend over and wiggle their bottoms. Passengers on the moon sometimes do the same, although this is not encouraged. Moon miffles paint faces on their bottoms which many people find amusing. Some print letters on their bottoms that spell words as you move down the track.

The Mooning Festival takes place annually on the 1st March and always takes place at night, as the temperature is cooler. Train tickets must be booked in advance and all tourists are advised to bring a torch, as little will be seen without one. Photographs are not permitted.

The Quiet Festival

The Quiet Festival is a festival with a difference and certainly not the place to go if you like to let your hair down. All participants attend the festival to experience the peace of quiet.

You can expect a wide range of activities, from meditation to mime artists, silent theatre, staring competitions and signing workshops. No noise is tolerated, not even whispers.

Children love the festival because the air is filled with butterflies from all over the moon. The final day of the festival is devoted to silent pin dropping where participants dress up as church mice and compete for the Silence is Golden award.

Zone 983 is the place to go if you want to get away from it all and experience silence at its best with like-minded souls. The Quiet Festival is held before the storm season begins.

The Festival of 8

On the 8th day of the 8th month at eight minutes past eight people meet in Crater 8 to celebrate all things 8. The number 8 has special significance on the moon because the number 8 on its side is the symbol for infinity. Eight is the number of days in a week, according to ancient moon people and it is the number of vertices a cube has.

Some moon people believe that the moon was born from a moon cube 8 billion years ago and the vertices still protect us from harm. On the day of Festival 8, the 8th black moon that orbits the moon changes colour 8 times and this sends everyone into frenzy. This only happens for 8 seconds, but people find it exhilarating.

People dance in circles of 8 and perform 8 rotations clockwise and then 8 rotations anticlockwise as 8 giant fireworks are let off. People dress up in 8 different colours and always attend in groups of 8. The food is sensational, with 8 courses every mealtime. With 8 different performances every night, you won't be short of things to do.

The Spinning Orb Festival

The Spinning Orb Festival takes place in the Crater of Dreams around Lake Bliss once a year, although many wish it could be every day. Here you will witness one of the most amazing spectacles anywhere in the solar system, as hundreds of magical orbs fly from Neptune every July and head for the moon.

People stand around Lake Bliss in the middle of the night and wait for the orbs to come. The expectation is enormous, and the waiting seems to take forever. Then hundreds of glowing white orbs descend from the night sky and enter moon air space at remarkable speed. They look as if they will smash into the lake, but they come to a stop in such dramatic fashion the audience gasps. The orbs then stop glowing and float majestically about 3m above the water's surface, frustratingly out of reach.

For five minutes, the orbs float almost without movement and then hundreds of sparks fly inside each orb and they begin to change colour. Spectators go wild with excitement as the orbs move around the lake – slowly at first, then faster and faster, spinning, twisting, and turning; all without colliding. The orbs dazzle spectators with their wonderful colours and astonishing movements for about an hour.

People are rooted to the spot, not once daring to look away. Then the orbs fly, one by one, into the sky and disappear into space as fast as they came, back to Neptune with a flourish. No one knows why the orbs choose to come to the moon, but we are glad that they do and we hope that every July they continue to come.

The Marbles Festival

The Marbles Festival, held in May each year, isn't what it seems. People attending the event as competitors bring six marbles with them. The marbles are given to the event organisers, who place them into a giant bucket. By the time everyone has handed in their marbles, the bucket contains over 20,000 marbles. The marbles are then fed into a giant marble canon and they are then blasted into open moon countryside.

Contestants are then given up to 29 hours to find their marbles. The winner is the first person to find all six of their marbles. The competition gets harder each year because marbles from previous years are never collected in. This means there are thousands and thousands of marbles everywhere.

Players attempt to make their marbles stand out from the crowd by painting them different colours, but even then, they are hard to see – and the terrain isn't that friendly, so even if marbles are brightly coloured, some may have landed in mud or disappeared into quicksand.

Most people leave the festival declaring they have lost their marbles. The prize for the winner, if there is one, is a talking marble. If you think a marble that talks is a remarkable thing, then you'd be right. They are incredible, so much so they are banned from taking part in festivals, because they can obviously shout your name and help you find them.

BOOKS

Reading is very important on the moon, which is why there are so many bookshops here. You'll notice that moon people always have their noses buried in a book. This can make the pages quite sticky, because moon people have quite runny noses. Now you know why books on the moon smell of honey and have lots of pages stuck together.

Moon people like holding books for enjoyment. They try to carry a couple of books for a week and just enjoy the anticipation of what might be inside. This explains why so many moon people look excited. It's because they are.

Not opening a book can be excruciating, but the expectation is universally recognised as being good for the brain, as it stimulates the wonder cells. If moon people can hold onto a book for a full seven days without peeking inside, then they are full of wonder and so become wonderful. This is the best time to read. If you read a book before becoming wonderful, it's not a problem – it just means you don't enjoy the book as much.

Being wonderful lasts for about three hours, which is fine as it takes a moon person about an hour to read a 900-page book, leaving two full hours to enjoy a feeling of magnificence. In this time, most moon people just sit and draw whatever comes into their heads. This is called flapdoodling.

When Moon people flapdoodle they use nozzle-noodles, squid-wiggles and sprocket-dollops. The pictures created are nothing less than brilliant but they are always thrown onto a fire when finished. No one knows why we do this but we do. It's just the way it is and has been since time began.

Moon people are ambidextrous readers, which mean they can read two books written in different languages at the same time. The left eye reads one book and the right eye reads another. The eyes rotate in their sockets after every sentence.

Some moon people like to read just one book at a time, but the principle is the same – the left eye reads the right page and the right eye reads the left page. Moon people can also read one book upside down and another downside up. We are also amphibious readers, which means we can read underwater and on land.

When moon people, read their eyelashes fall out. Don't worry, though, as they grow back again and normally pretty quickly. It used to be the case that when a moon person read a book, their toenails would grow, and they would have to take their shoes off.

Thankfully someone read a book about how to stop this from happening and so people can now read with their shoes on. This book was found by accident after a book shower by someone who tripped over it whilst taking their fluorescent shoes for a walk.

Reading is only something moon people can do at certain altitudes. For example, reading inside a canyon causes moon people to vomit because there is a build-up of lunapooze bubbles in their blood vessels, a moon gas that can be fatal. This also happens in gorges, valleys, dales, and glens.

The worst place to read a book is inside a moon crater tunnel. This leads to hysteria, sickness and eventually word combustion. From an Earth telescope, this might appear as a bright white spot. It's actually someone blowing up.

It may interest you to know that moon people can read in the dark. Basically, our eyes can store light and retrieve it when needed. This is a very useful gift and ideal for midnight book feasts and early morning book parties.

Moon people have the same eyesight capabilities as mantis shrimps, found on the Great Barrier Reef of Australia, Earth. Moon people, like the shrimps, can see in 12 primary colours, whereas humans can see only three.

Reading without the lights on isn't all that great, though, if the book you are reading has an author who's afraid of the dark. There is nothing worse than opening a book up to find an author trembling behind a long paragraph. Some words hate the dark, too, which makes things even worse, because they can scream themselves silly until you put a light on. This is why we don't tend to read in the dark very much.

Before the age of seven, children read talking books. They love them. Each page of a talking book is covered in the author's face and the words of the book are printed over the face. The author reads the words as they are supposed to be read, so full expression is guaranteed. The author helps to read tricky words and even interacts with the reader, asking questions and sharing ideas along the way.

Authors are very cunning. They will check that you are reading with them by reading words that aren't on the page. If you don't spot them doing this, then they will know you haven't been concentrating and will shout really loudly to wake you up. A sincere apology is normally enough to get an author back on your side, but they won't be pleased if you do it again.

Talking books will read and read and read all day long if you don't close them. This isn't something the authors like because it gives them a sore throat. They also find it extremely rude, because they think no one is listening.

This isn't true, of course, because the wallpaper soaks up every single word and breathes them all out at night when everyone is asleep. The words crawl up your nose and splash into your dreams without you knowing. When they've had enough, they dry themselves on a vowel.

All books on the moon can talk, but some prefer not to if they don't like the look of the person reading them. You can read a book without the author reading to you if you prefer. On the spine of the book is a zip. Pull it up and this closes the author's mouth. This means that when you read a book, the author just stares at you. Some people find this quite off-putting and so pull the zip down.

Some authors are very rude and if they don't like the look of you, then they won't read a word. Don't let this put you off, because some authors just take time to get to know their readers. You will find that if you persevere, then an author might suddenly start reading halfway through the book. If this happens, it is best not to make a fuss but just carry on reading as if nothing has happened. By the end of the book, an author becomes great friends with its reader.

However, some authors never speak. They might pull faces at you or stick their tongue out, which really isn't on. If your author does this, then then take your book back to the shop where you purchased it and ask for a refund. If you borrowed it from a library, just tell the librarians that the author has been rude. They will normally ban the book from the library if they receive more than three complaints, and the book is thrown on a word dump.

Moon people are prolific readers, especially children. By the time they can walk word tightropes, moon children will have read over 10,000 books including:

The Laughing Galaxy
Gravity Sucks
Galactic Gobs
The Parachuting Planets
Cosmic Soups and Cosmic Poops
Wobbly Universes
Meet the Meteorites
Time to Warp
Space Toys Fight Back
The Leaking Miracles of Universe 4

Anything read is tattooed on the brain forever and cannot be forgotten. Moon people have 'dolphin' memories. These are a thousand times more powerful than an elephant's. If you don't believe me, test them. Pick any book a moon person has read, go to any page and ask them to recite the page. They will not only narrate the page to you word perfectly, but they will also tell you how many commas and full stops there are.

Moon people will often rewrite a book if they think they can make a better job of it than the author. They will even tell an author this as the book is being read to them. You can try this for yourself. If you don't like what an author says in reply, then go outside and leave the book in the wind so all words are blown off the page.

Open books have the problem of words escaping. When this happens, runaway words find a new book and climb inside a sentence they like the look of. These words can go unnoticed for years and some are never found again, especially adjectives. A simile in the wrong place sticks out like a sore thumb, though, and they have a tough job taking cover.

Authors don't like words to abscond, because it can make reading confusing. When a whole page of words decide they've had enough, then things really can get messy, particularly if they kidnap one of the characters.

Some words choose not to escape. They rearrange themselves on a page instead, because they like the look of the author's face getting tongue-tied trying to read the words. Some words are so full of mischief they will print themselves backwards or move letters as they are being read. An author hates this because it makes their mouth turn to mush and they can choke on their own words.

Sometimes words stay exactly where they are, but mess around with their punctuation, putting commas, full stops, semi-colons, colons, exclamation marks, question marks, and speech marks in random places. Some paragraphs throw out every scrap of punctuation altogether.

Many moon people are good at reading between the lines. We are also pretty good at reading above and under lines. We see things there that others can't. There are often more words in between lines than there are actual words on a page. This is where most of an author's juiciest thoughts are and they are normally sandwiched between slices of ideas. Some have quite deep fillings when you start looking. Some can be a bit cheesy, some a bit chewy, but others can really tickle your taste buds.

Books don't like being stacked on top of each other especially the books towards the bottom of a pile. The words get squashed and opening a page of squashed words isn't a pretty sight. It looks like a graveyard of swatted flies. Vowels leak yellow and consonants tend to ooze a brown juice like octopus ink.

People that have read a squashed book complain that their sense of smell has been paralysed as a result and that their eyeballs sting. To keep a book and its words in perfect condition, it is always best to store them upright in dry ice. Not enough moon people do this, which is why dry ice books are so collectable.

There's something else that a book and its talking author don't like and that is being closed really hard. This can lead to word concussion and really painful headaches that take weeks to recover from. When a book is opened up again, don't be at all surprised to find an author looking terrible. Some closed books have to be rushed to a word hospital to have paragraph-threatening word clots removed.

Moon people are very particular about their books. When you go into a bookshop or library, you will find that books by male and female authors are never placed next to each other unless they are married. You'd be surprised how many authors are married to each other.

If a book has two authors, one male and one female and they aren't married, this causes chaos, because bookshops have nowhere to put them. These books normally have to be ordered. A book with multiple authors is just ridiculous and not encouraged on the moon.

If you are an Earth tourist, you'd also be surprised to find that books on the moon are all written in invisible ink. Visit a moon bookshop and you'll see row upon row of what look like books with no titles and empty pages. Don't be fooled. They are heaving with the most delightful words ever written.

Moon people have no trouble reading invisible ink, but it can be confusing for non-moon people. There is nothing funnier than watching distant friends flicking through a moon book in total befuddlement. They often have the books upside-down, which makes it even more hilarious. We don't laugh outwardly, though – we store the laugh in our brains and let it out when we get home, as we don't like to offend anyone.

Tourists can buy books and have them dipped in translating water, which removes the invisible ink. The water is special dry water, so none of the pages get wet. You will notice that a lot of our books have detachable mirrors in the back. This is to help you read the words, as everything is printed in reverse. Book mirrors aren't all the same, though. Some only work on storybooks and others have been designed so that they won't reflect anything if held to a particular author.

You won't find second-hand books on the moon, only second-hand clocks and second thoughts. Books take great offence at being second best to anything, so don't bother looking for used books, as they are not officially recognised. A book remains new even if it is old, because someone who has never read it sees it for the first time, so it is by definition a novel experience.

Moon people like to cuddle up with a good book whenever they can. Good books contain lots of cosy words and these make us feel safe. Books feel the same way. They like to be cuddled.

It is ill mannered to leave a book on a bookshelf for too long, gathering moon dust. They have a shelf life of about 500 years, after which some turn into condensation. Some are eaten by their authors.

Books that are kept on shelves don't like going on the end of a row, because the view doesn't tend to be as good. Bookends also have a terrible reputation for falling asleep whilst working and so end of row books worry non-stop about falling from wuthering heights. If they do fall then they almost certainly end up with spinal damage. Being on the end of a row of books is the equivalent of being on death row for a book.

Inside the spine of every book you will find a bookworm and a long feather duster. These wiggly wonders polish dusty words if a book hasn't been read for a while, and they make sure that any dog-eared pages are pulled back and ironed out.

Bookworms that live in children's books really have their work cut out, because the pages are under constant attack from crayon, felt tips, paw prints and food. Some pages also get ripped, which bookworms find a real bind to repair. Contrary to popular belief, bookworms do not wear glasses. They wear loud shorts and quiet shirts. They aren't that fussed about reading, either, as they don't really have the time. They also can't read, which makes matters worse.

Books are written in such a way that when you finish one, you can turn it upside down and read a different story to the one you have just read. That's because all our words make new words when read from a different angle.

When a moon person has had enough of reading a book, they might throw it very hard into the air. A moon person's throw is sufficient to send the book into space, and off it goes for someone else to read in another part of space.

Moon people believe that books are for sharing. Books launched into space could, of course, end up anywhere, which is all part of the fun. People on other moons do the same thing, which is why space is actually full of books and not meteorites as Earth people think.

During certain times of the year, we experience book showers. These are books from all the vertices of the omniverse. They often fall at the most inappropriate times and they can be quite dangerous, especially if they are hardback.

For example, last year two 5kg books fell through the roof of a cosmic hallway in the Cuboid Museum, injuring three tourists. 5kg might not sound like very much, but say it as 5,000g and you'll find that's pretty heavy. It's the weight of a young moon dog!

On the positive side, though, we have books written in languages we have never seen before, and we employ thousands of moon people to study them who try to work out what they mean. These people are called moon crackers.

Most moon people own a book written from another world, but very few people own a book written from another world with illustrations. If you find one of these books, then you are very lucky indeed. An illustrated book is a highly prized item and worth a fortune.

For every book written on the moon, there are three thrown on a word dump. These are the drafts of published books and contain all sorts of scribbling, crossings-out, doodles, drink stains, and words that didn't quite make the grade.

Open word dumps have become a problem in some parts of the moon. These sprawling areas of word waste are dirty and dangerous places where moon mig birds pick and poke at leftover adjectives and adverbs.

This is where you will find some children, too, working as word scavengers for unscrupulous wordsmiths picking up words with their bare hands. They sift through discarded sentences, surplus paragraphs, unwanted poems, and forgotten stories looking for parts of words they can stick together or for ideas they can steal. The wordsmith then sells them to unsuspecting authors struggling for inspiration.

Children collect words in the daytime, using sacks called language bags. At night, they glue the words together using a special language adhesive to make them look like words that have been in the dictionary for years.

Some of them can be quite convincing, such as wiggywit, fizzdonkle, spox-twang, nazzgrapper, goop-hubber, kipbipper, chuzz-dacking, bixyoddling, pizzlunking, yezzneffer, and pagnaffer.

Most of the words they collect and join together have no value or meaning, so to be worth anything they have to be given a convincing definition. For example:

chuzz-dacking, *verb*. The act of chasing a moon pancake back into its hole.

yezzneffer, *noun*. A soulless, angry and featherless bird that wears mustard coloured socks and a red scarf.

spox-twang, *verb*. The act of clumping a flitch-nibble until it falls about laughing and wees itself.

The problem is, a lot of word scavengers don't always understand the words they are reading. They end up collecting words, phrases and yarns that can often be toxic, such as street slang and horror stories.

It has been a major concern on the moon that children working on the dumps often find offensive words and hurtful ideas and start using them without knowing what they are really saying. Inevitably, they attract trouble.

In order to get round this, moon scientists are hoping to magnetise these words so that they can be easily detected and crushed. Open word dumps are a sight we would rather you not see. If you do, then we guarantee you will be lost for words.

The popularity of books changes all the time on the moon, but at the time of writing the Top Ten Moon Books are as follows:

Total Eclipse of the Mind
Focus Pocus
The Universe is a Pigeon
Remote-controlled Space Pumpkins
Space Wrinkles and Memory Transplants
Lunatic Clouds and Insane Winds
Watch this Space

The Revenge of the Furry Planets
Origami Universes and Magnetic Nightmares
Spitting Space Socks

These books have all been written by the same author, too: Maze, a moon writer from Zone 29. She writes a book a day and is our most prolific author. Her most famous title is The Blowing Star and the Smiling Moon, which has been translated into 46,000 different languages.

There are plenty of books that have been banned on the moon, as well, including:

Moon Cows
When the Omniverse Stubbed Its Toe
Galactic Cannibalism
The Edge of Space
Sleeping in the Shade of a Cosmic Secret
The Headless Nebula
The Migraine Stars
When Space Popped Sideways

Books mostly get banned because they are rubbish and the words inside stink. Some books get banned because their authors ask to be expelled from the moon, so they become famous. This tends to backfire, because the words inside their books rot and so no one ever reads them. They end up as space manure.

Bookmarks are also banned on the moon. They tend to live up to their name and leave grubby marks all over a page and are terrible for smudging words.

Just a word of warning: if you have a habit of licking your finger and thumb before turning a page, then beware of reading a book from Venus or Mercury because the pages are poisonous. Book-related deaths are rare, but they can happen. We are trying to get books with poisonous pages banned, but they are not easy to spot until it's too late.

QUESTIONS

Moon people are often called 'down to Earth' folk that like to ask all sorts of interesting questions and post them in other people's letter boxes. They will post them in anyone's letter box and not just to someone they know.

If you receive a question it is polite to write a reply even if you don't know the answer and then bury it in the garden for the wurdles to read.

Wurdles are intelligent worms who keep themselves to themselves and love eating words, especially their own. If your answer is correct then wurdles will gobble and guzzle it up. Any answers that are wide of the mark are left to decay in the rich moon soil where the words breakdown into vowels and consonants for gibblesnippers to crunch. This means that virtually all the questions we want answering are literally beneath our feet inside a wurdle somewhere.

You might ask why we don't dig wurdles up to get at the answers but that would be madness. Wurdles don't like the light and if they are exposed to even a squint of it they turn inside out, which erases everything they know. We tend to think that asking a question is so much more satisfying than knowing the answer.

Some of the questions moon people ask might seem barkingly batty and ludicrously loopy to you but they are things moon people really want to know the answers to and they will think about them a lot. Here are some examples of the sorts of things we think about:

- Are drawing pins afraid of whistles with chicken-pox?
- How many scarecrows are travelling on flying carpets at any one time?
- What do rainbows taste like after their sell-by-date?
- Is codswallop more dangerous than claptrap?
- Do marbles have déjà vu?
- Is the dark afraid of the light going out?
- Would you expect to see a sandstorm inside a snow frog?
- Is the glue on the back of a stamp happy?
- Why don't Earth people spread toad vomit on their toast?
- What question do questions get sick of being asked?
- When would you expect to see a magic pen cry?
- Who asks the questions when the alphabet dissolves?
- Does lipstick ever get stage fright?
- Why do windows under anaesthetic still feel pain?
- Do echoes sleepwalk?
- What do hairy balloons have in common with tambourine picnics?
- Are mummified anchors safe?
- Why do idea extensions smell so stale?
- Do fish fish?
- How do hens lay eggs with the dates printed on them?

- If a dressing gown could talk what would it say to its belt?
- What happens to exhausted peas when they cross the finishing line?
- Is it better to be outside in or inside out?

Moon people can't stop asking questions because one good question always leads to another. On average they probably ask about 100 questions every 5 minutes. These are all different types.

For example, moon people might ask themselves prickly questions. These sorts of questions tend to be quite spiky and they have a habit of scratching the mind and puncturing stray brain cells.

Prickly questions you might cut yourself on include:

- Why don't forgotten toenails cry in space?
- Is a moon monkey's raincoat really up to the job?
- What happens if a word in your ear can't get out?
- What do secrets with vertigo think about when they are vacuuming phobias?
- Do dead batteries need a light on at night?
- Does the soul of an apple crunch when it is asleep?
- Do fish see the point?
- Do pigs pull ham strings?
- Is the colour wheel just a pigment of your imagination?
- When does enough know when it has had enough?
- What is the difference between a climple-pot and a clomple-pit?
- Does the tip of an ice-berg ever wish it wasn't?
- If you tickle the sides of the universe how long will it laugh for?

- How much does your imagination weigh?
- Why don't cows jump over Jupiter's moons?
- Do questions with a twist wear knickers?
- Is boiled rice more unpredictable at night?
- What happens to kangaroo poo lost in space?

Prickly questions should be asked in a serious tone of voice with a sharp frown and the head tilted slightly one way. This helps move the words from one side of the brain to the other. Some people put a finger and thumb to their face when they think like this.

Someone might ask you a canny question when you are on the moon. Canny questions are annoying sorts of questions that tend to get a bit too big for their boots. Don't worry if you can't answer them because they can't even answer themselves.

Canny questions you could trip over include:

- Can underwater hairdryers tie shoelaces?
- Can the colour green go red with embarrassment?
- Can a whisper shout?
- Can an igloo catch fire?
- Can a match box?
- Can you kill one stone with two birds?
- Can blind horses cook miracles?
- Can waterproof teabags throw dice on an empty stomach?
- Can a galactic gugganut snore memories through greaseproof paper?
- Can a trapped nerve count to 100 without a pom-pup interrupting?
- Can you get cornered in a round room?
- Can you be a closet claustrophobic?

- Can a scrambled egg poach its feelings?
- Can a humble genius climb inside ignorance without getting covered in wet paint?
- Can silence hear itself think?
- Can a whistle freeze a hum without burning its fingers?
- Can nightmares have daydreams?
- Can a pinch steal a nip?
- Can smells hear feelings?
- Can a pointless question digest an idea in freezing fog?

Canny questions are normally asked with outstretched arms and a look of bewilderment mixed with a heavy dose of sarcasm. They are best asked with no real intention and whilst walking away from the person you are speaking to.

Then there are fluffy questions. These tend to be harmless questions with a soft belly and a heart of gold. The question marks tend to be made of marshmellow. A fluffy question might be:

- How does a jacket potato feel without buttons?
- How many feathers cry their hearts out inside a duvet at night?
- Does an orange really have to be squashed to extract its juice?
- If you turn over a new leaf do the other leaves get upset?
- When gravity gets depressed, how does it pick itself up again?
- Do hard feelings have soft hands?
- Do the bristles on a toothbrush worry about being pulled out?

- What happens to a wishing well when it has run dry of wishes?
- Does it hurt the tube when squeezing toothpaste?
- Does a pillow fight find it funny?
- What is it really like to be a conker?

Fluffy questions focus mainly on feelings and they should always be asked with a look of worried sincerity. Eyes should be widened and eyebrows should be raised. Neither should be very dramatic. Moon people who ask fluffy questions like to get together to discuss them. They don't get very far though as they tend to feed each other with even more anxiety. They often need counselling.

There are then just plain silly questions which even moon people find daft. Examples include:

- Is it safe to unpeel a banana when it is sleeping?
- How many cuckoos does it take to change a light bulb?
- If you can squash an orange why can't you squash a brown?
- How many dominoes can you fit in a coffin?
- Does a mirror have a colourful soul?
- Do cobwebs get tired of waiting?
- Why does your nose run and where does it run to?
- Where do panic buttons go to relax?
- If all the germs living on Neptune burped at the same time, would this wake up the gridgrax sleeping in wide space?
- Do radiowaves wear slippers?
- Do blades of grass know where they are?
- Why were full stops banned from playing hide and seek?

- What happens if you wake up and find yourself inside a dictionary?

Moon people love to experiment with their thoughts. This is called mind munching. When they think of a question they start to slowly chew it over in their minds. If brain cells get excited then the mind throws the question from side to side and gives it a good chomp.

Some questions can be quite gristly and so have to be mentally spat out. When a moon person thinks of an answer to a question, then the answer has the job of trying to get out. Lots of answers find this quite a challenge and they can remain inside heads for years. This is because their brains contain so many mazes and as soon as an answer has found its way out of one maze, it steps into another.

Some answers get lost and forgotten about. These lonely souls can sometimes cause headaches as they bang on the walls of mind mazes crying to get out. When they stop banging, so does the headache.

Ideas can also be found wandering the corridors of mind mazes. Some reach dead ends and just sit there. Others never give up and keep on the move. As they dart around it is not uncommon for solitary ideas to bump into each other and team up. When this happens the moon person they belong to often twitches and has something called a mind sneeze and the ideas fly out.

Moon people get migraines just like Earth people except we know why they really happen. They are connected to trains of thought. When a moon person is thinking hard about a question then a train of thought develops. As the train moves through the brain it picks up lots of passengers. These passengers are ideas and they each carry luggage which are packed with words.

The problem is, when a moon person thinks about a problem or a question for too long the train gets faster and faster until eventually it derails. This causes a real mess inside a moon person's head because all the carriages end up crashing into each other. The ideas and their luggage get thrown about and there are nouns, adjectives, adverbs and verbs everywhere. This is the pain we call a migraine.

As you move from zone to zone on the moon you are likely to see circles of moon people holding hands with each other. These are known as question circles. They are not planned, they just happen.

It starts with someone who stands in an open space with both arms outstretched. This is recognised by all moon people as an invitation to hold hands in order to question share. After a while, a couple of people will join hands and so the circle grows. There is no limit to the size of the circle but they tend to be about 8-10 moon people. When a circle has been formed, everyone starts to move and moon people take it in turns to speak their minds by asking a question as the circle rotates. The rest of the circle then offer their ideas and share what they think.

Moon people believe that as the circle moves, this moves people's minds to find answers. Question circles last for as long as they last, normally until someone needs the toilet and the circle is broken and becomes a wavy line.

Another way moon people share their ideas is to enter thought bubbles. You'll see these mostly in the big cities and they look like giant balloons with a door. If you have a question tap dancing on your mind then a thought bubble is the place to go. You walk in, sit down and say what you need to say to a mirror above you. This looks like an ordinary mirror but your reflection listens to what you have to say and then replies. This is weird for those new to a thought bubble because when you talk your reflection doesn't move its lips. When you stop talking your reflection starts to talk.

It can be quite an experience to talk to yourself and have yourself talk back to you. Sometimes we even tell ourselves the right answer. This tells us that we are able to solve our own problems and that the answer to all our questions can be found inside us.

It is worth pointing out that thought bubbles aren't the answer to everything. They often give the wrong information out. They do this deliberately because they have a mischievous side to them.

Sometimes they just sit there and pull a funny face. In order to get at the right answer, you yourself have to be in a good mood. If you are, your reflection is more likely to treat you seriously.

A lot of moon people will complain because they can't hear themselves think. That's normally because they bombard their heads with so many questions that they have multiple conversations going on at the same time.

Ideas can spend ages chatting to each other and sometimes in the most inconvenient of places. If they get engrossed in trying to answer a question they tend to stand in the doorways of thought corridors and this prevents other ideas from getting by even if they do say excuse me.

When ideas get tunnel vision and don't see what's going on around them or if they refuse to budge then we normally lose the ability to think straight. This leads to mind fog which won't clear unless someone sucks it out with a mind vac. This is exactly like a vacuum cleaner but a mini version that has two nozzles. A high setting is normally required to get a head clear again.

If a mind vac doesn't work then a visit to the pharmacy is needed where we can buy mind solution. A slurp of this three times an hour for two hours helps pop questions and unblocks troublesome ideas. These appear as little flashes in the eyes. Questions that are popped are lost forever which isn't as bad as it sounds because some of the questions are real posers.

Mind solution is out of the question for extinguishing any burning questions though. A bucket of cold water thrown in the face is the only thing that works in this situation.

Thinking outside the box isn't something moon people do a lot of. We find questions tend to go a bit free-range and lose the plot. We prefer instead to think inside triangular prisms or in pyramids where the air is cleaner and we can keep an eye on our ideas. Thinking inside a box is not recommended as there are no windows and thoughts can go stale.

People that say there are two sides to every question haven't been to the moon. These 'pancake thinkers' have a very flat view of the omniverse. We think that a question probably has at least 100 sides to it, which is why it helps to be good at maths when answering one, even if the question itself has nothing to do with maths. We think that if a question can be answered then it can't really be a good question.

Although moon people ask loads of questions, we do struggle to think of them from time to time. Questions are harder to come by after a meal of niffballs, or being chased by a pink swan or watching a queue grow a longer tail.

We also find that questions tend to hide from our imaginations when we are walking through tunnels or tying our shoelaces in the dark. To get a question out in the open sometimes requires a lot of mind squeezing. This is a bit like pencil squeezing when you are stuck on a problem; you squeeze really hard and hope the right answer comes out.

Mind squeezing is the same. You scrunch up your face and hope that a question emerges covered in wonder. What you normally get is something covered in treacle that tends to squiff! You could ask someone else to try and help you mind squeeze but this tends to be painful if they squeeze too hard.

Some moon people find that hours of mind squeezing doesn't get them anywhere apart from more frustrated so they go and squeeze something else instead. Moon people like squeezing poems about towels, riddles about dead butterflies, songs about moon-hops and snail monologues.

If we are still dry of questions after a week then a trip to the doctor normally does the trick. The doctor asks us loads of questions and then prescribes a course of question patches to help get things moving. These small round patches are the size of a fingernail and we wear them on our temples as this is where most questions are made.

The question patches release a lot of question marks into the bloodstream and these head off in search of lost ideas. When a question mark has found an idea it will feed it and give it plenty of water as they tend to be quite dehydrated and a bit unsteady on their feet. After a few days the ideas pick up strength and before long they are back to full steam and running again. Questions tend to come thick and fast then.

When a question does eventually emerge from its chrysalis then we experience a feeling similar to when the penny drops. This is a bit like walking on water, seeing the light, and flying without wings. Everything is fine unless we experience a question avalanche and then we get snowed under again.

If you head over to Crater 321 then pay a visit to the amazing moon mind-quarium. This is just like a fish aquarium but is home to thousands of thoughts that swim about inside large spinning think tanks. If you have ever wondered what a thought looks like, then the mind-quarium is the place to see one.

Thoughts come in many different sizes and the various think tanks on show let you view everything from little tiddlers to big ideas. The thoughts are kept in a special mind juice from the Sage Ocean of the Northern Hemisphere. This is fed directly into the mind-quarium.

During a visit you will come face to face with mindlife from every part of the moon including trivial thoughts such as, 'Why do my toes hurt?' to incredible thoughts such as, 'Does iron in the bloodstream go rusty if you leave the tap running?'

From the hidden minds of moon people, the mind-quarium transports visitors to the spectacular underwater mindshafts of Crater 321 and the simple beauty of shallow mind waters – home to everything from failed inventions, bungles, tell-tales and frauds to mind flashes, visions, brainstorms and ground-breaking ideas.

Other displays reveal the diversity of the thinking world with naturally themed mind-maps, tropical mind jungles, and fast-moving mind mash habitats alongside open-top ideas, thought caves, thought walkways and dream bridges.

Questions like to run around in the playground of our minds and some don't stop even when we have blown the whistle. Some of these questions might not have heard the whistle whereas some are just naughty and so are made to stand by the fence.

These questions are ones that pretend not to listen and always answer back. Examples of belligerent questions include:

- Why?
- Will the wind fizz if you keep it prisoner in a bottle of dreams?
- Can a pigeon fly in and out of your head without a passport?
- Do camels float?
- How can moon dogs drink from mirages and hear their smells?
- What happens to squishy words that capsize?
- Are we there yet?
- Is that your real face?
- Is it?
- Am I here?

Without question, belligerent questions can get very annoying because they repeat themselves over and over again until you are ready to burst. Some just don't stop. If this happens then we chat with a friend who might be prepared to swap one of their annoying questions. What's irritating to one person often isn't to somebody else.

Swapping questions is very common on the moon and it's something you might like to try when you get here. One thing you must do when you are here though and that is question everything... we expect nothing less.

PRESENTS

Moon people like to give presents by stealth. You might wake up one morning to find a cloud above your house and not have the faintest clue who gave it to you. The cloud follows you for the whole day, whatever you are doing. A cloud might not sound like a present but moon clouds are a bit different to Earth clouds.

Some moon clouds are pink and fluffy and they rain happiness onto you. This isn't rainwater, but tiny balls of candyfloss. These little spheres of bliss dissolve when they come into contact with you and the result is utter contentment, which can be quite long-lasting depending on the size of the cloud given.

Cloud givers like to remain anonymous and there is no way of tracing them, which makes things even more exciting. This means that anyone you meet on the moon could be the person who sent you a moon cloud. How wonderful.

Happy clouds are made to order by a factory inside the moon and are delivered when no one is looking. You might walk down the street and suddenly see a moon cloud about the size of a pancake appear above someone's head. It's lovely to see the change of expression on the person under the cloud. Their smile is something to behold, although photos are not permitted.

The great thing about a moon cloud is that even though you might not get one yourself, if you see one, they make you smile, too. Imagine being under one. You could be soon.

Giving presents is something moon people love doing even more than chewing the toenails of quifflequicks. If you are on the moon for more than a few days, then you're pretty likely to get a present from someone. It's the way we do things here.

The present you receive might not be something you want, and we can't guarantee that you will like it. Moon presents can be more than a little odd.

In one month, it wouldn't be unusual to receive Siamese bloodsucking pentagons, a ball filled with vinegar, a magnetic field, a timezone from Venus, diamond dust, a black hole, a schizophrenic French-speaking kitten, a grain of Mars salt, some carrot jam, a pair of opera glasses, a coffee drawing, a bolt of lightning, the false teeth of a tishnink, a wigwam made of bees' wings and a nervous horseshoe.

Moon people always keep a present given to them, even if it is something that has no obvious use. Moon people believe that all presents come in handy at some time in their lives. You might not realise how useful something is until years after it was given to you.

Imagine waking up one morning and finding on your doorstep a yodelling sound inside a transparent egg. What do you do with it? You might think that the best place to keep a yodelling sound is inside a sock, and you'd be right! They are safe in there. After a while you might be tempted to crack it open, but something tells you not to.

Now imagine that a few years later, your washing machine stops working and refuses to wash your clothes. Imagine it won't open its door and posts a notice saying,

'All clothes will be kept prisoner until further notice.' This would be a nightmare if your best clothes were in there, pleading to be let out. When you read the instructions to the washing machine, you discover that this is an extremely rare malfunction and the only thing that can repair the problem is to pour a yodelling sound into its top drawer.

So you crack open the egg, pour it into the washing machine drawer and wait. At first, nothing seems to happen, but then you hear something singing inside the machine. There are lots of giggles, too, and before you know it, the washer is spinning again and your clothes are done and released without harm. The side effect of this is that your clothes now sing when you wear them, which make them great party clothes.

You later find out that yodelling sounds are so rare that to order another one from the manufacturer would take 419 years, because they have to come from the other side of the Milky Way.

This simple tale has a moral: never give a moon present away, never throw one away and don't even think about selling one. Not even if you are given lice from an emu or a stuffed mirage.

A moon present could save your life. The only time this doesn't apply is when a moon horse gives you a gift. Don't accept it. Just run.

Some of the presents we receive are not always obvious as gifts. Every new day is a present to moon people. We say that yesterday is the past, tomorrow is the future and today is a gift, which is why we call it the present.

Some presents are so well-disguised, they are harder to spot than mossy leaftailed lugnuns. For example, you might be on the receiving end of a kind word or a piece of advice. At the time, you might not see it as much of a present, but they are normally wrapped in layers of compassion with a big bow of love on the top.

Because advice doesn't cost anything, most people try to give some word parcels as a present. Some of these parcels need more unwrapping than others. See if you can get your head around this little sackful:

- Don't eat too many dreams or your mind will put on weight.
- Don't let your past steal your future. If it does, then ask for a refund.
- Head space is a good place to visit, but don't stay there too long.
- If the red crow croaks before midnight, then the silence will sing for its breakfast.
- Slow fires make nightmares sweat quickly.
- Cover your castle in jam and watch the flies change direction.
- When the cave elephants awaken, then your luck will roll uphill.
- Wrap your ideas in a yellow blanket if you want them to grow tall.
- Climb inside a dream and find a nightmare falling outside.
- A wise fish will always be out of water carrying an umbrella.
- If you can't see the bright side, don't worry because it's not there.
- A shadow that moves at the speed of light should never be kept in the dark.

- If someone steals your ladder, take the necessary steps.
- When you draw the curtains at night, always use a sharp pencil.

When moon people receive presents, they don't always open them. They enjoy the thought of what might be inside and just look at them. Some people are so good at delaying the opening ceremony that they don't unwrap presents for years. They squirrel them away until they are ready. Even when they do get round to opening their packets and parcels, they do so very slowly. They might start opening one corner of a present on a Monday, then walk away from it, returning the next night to rip a bit more of the paper.

People who live by the motto 'there's no time like the present' simply cannot do this. If the present is there, it soon sheds its skin. They unwrap faster than a retractable chord disappearing into a vacuum cleaner.

The very idea of a past present gathering dust is a crime to their way of thinking. And the idea of unwrapping a present in stages over the course of a week is plain madness.

Presents are given all the time on the moon, except on someone's birthday. That's a special day and a gift in itself, so no one bothers and it would be rude to interfere. Presents are given for no particular reason, other than that it's a fun thing to do.

Don't worry if you don't receive a present, either. It's not because you are unpopular or smell too much. It's just that sometimes you get them and sometimes you don't. If some people look like they are getting presents all the time, then don't worry about that either.

There's nothing worse than being present tense. People that seemingly get presents all the time don't get them forever. Your turn comes soon enough. It's a bit like pass the parcel. Everyone gets something eventually. If you complain about not getting any presents, then it doesn't change anything. You still have to wait.

Presents are all around us, anyway, and most of them don't have fancy wrapping paper. All we have to do is look. The Moon Mountains are a fantastic present. These majestic rock giants inspire thoughts of greatness and it is well known that paying regular visits to them can help you achieve something remarkable. What a treat. If this happens, then you end up inventing something fantastic that changes people's lives forever. Wow. If you haven't seen the Moon Mountains yet, then put it on your 'to-do' list and see how they make you feel. They are sure to gift you something.

Some moon people will go on present walks or present jogs. These involve following a particular route and discovering new things, old things and things in between. You'll find presents shouting your name if you look hard enough. A present might appear as a colour, a view or a smell. It might be an experience. They might be things you have walked by a hundred times before and not really appreciated or they might be things you never knew existed.

The present could be a new feeling, idea or question. For example, you might turn a corner and stumble across a tree with a trunk covered in hundreds of microchip boards, branches made of glowing glass and levitating moon apples. This fires a feeling of delight through your spine and makes your brain hairs stand on end. That's not a bad present to have.

You might see a legless table chasing a bottomless chair or a stringless guitar meditating with a keyless piano. This makes your eyebrows dance. That's a nice present to have, too. Or, if you are quiet, you might be lucky enough to hear the heartbeat of a pavement crack, cauliflowers clapping or false noses sneezing. Those presents are memory gold.

Moon people like to give presents to people they have never met, and gift capsules are a favourite gift for planting in the moonscape wildernesses and inside forests.

Gift capsules are interlocking orbs the size of footballs and they can hold a surprising amount of presents. People stuff their gift capsules with all sorts of treats. For example, you might find a recipe for toe cheese, a nest of jokes, a miniature shipwreck, a sky drum, the vocal chords of a stuttering hen, a karate chop, and some belly buttons.

If you plan on planting your own gift capsule, then you must remember to plant them when no one is looking and plant them at least 11m underground. Gift capsules cannot be detected except by intuition. They are not magnetic and they emit no signals. You just have to have a feeling where one is buried and go with your gut instincts. When you dig for a gift capsule the anticipation of finding one can be exhausting, so remember to pace yourself, and always take a friend.

Some people find what appear to be empty gift capsules, but they hardly ever are. It's because people don't know what they are looking at. The invisible gas inside a gift capsule might be something special, and without knowing it, you have already breathed it in and the gift is inside you.

Don't worry; all gases placed inside a gift capsule are harmless. Some gases are dream-based and others are composed of inspiration, ambition and invention. This explains why some people go on to be great thinkers or magic scientists.

Although many people like to give presents anonymously, many people love to give them face to face. You can do this in different ways. You might spend the day with a friend and hold onto their present for the whole time, taking it with you everywhere you go. Although this might seem cruel, it isn't because your friend will get even more excited wondering what is inside, and the present itself will almost burst in anticipation.

A popular way to give a present is to throw it at the person you are giving it to and then run off and turn around after about 50m and look at their reaction through a pair of binoculars as they open it.

Another way to give a gift involves kicking the shins of your recipient and slapping them in the face. Not really! What some people do is meet in the middle of an abandoned crater and give their friend a present through a present curtain. The recipient sits on one side of a table separated by a tall, wide pair of closed curtains, which hide a few friends and their presents. Someone then slowly moves a present through the curtains without being seen. The recipient opens the present and has to guess who it is from.

The curtains are designed so that friends can see through the closed curtains from their side, but the recipient cannot see from the other side. This means that friends get to see your reaction.

Some people opt to cover their presents in a self-wrapping paper. This is also self-unwrapping. Simply place your present on the paper and watch it fold itself around the object and stick itself down. Ribbons and bows are optional.

Self-wrapping papers are immaculate and look sensational, so much so that the lucky recipients are reluctant to open them. When the recipient is ready to open their present, all they have to do is place an outstretched hand on top for three seconds and it will unwrap in slow motion, revealing the gift inside bit by bit. Even people who are able to unwrap a present with their minds prefer a self-unwrapping present to open.

Some moon people don't like receiving presents because it makes them feel uncomfortable. They generally have an allergy to the giftwrap, which makes them itch and brings them out in spots.

If you give a present to someone who suddenly starts itching, then take it back immediately and throw a bucket of water on them as soon as you can.

There are an enormous amount of lost property presents on the moon. They tend to get left on trains or people put them down whilst being nosey and walk off without them.

Some of the more unusual presents that have been handed in include the nostril of a wig-wig bat, a pseudonym, a draught, a diseased yo-yo, an exploding golf ball, a plughole and a happy brick.

If a gift is not reclaimed after two years, then it is rewrapped and posted to different parts of the moon to random addresses. You will never know if the gift you receive is a lost property gift or not.

If you have lost a gift and you think you can prove that it is yours, then good luck. Most gifts are never reclaimed because the paperwork is a nightmare. Some people try to intentionally lose a gift if they think they won't have a use for it, but this is frowned upon by most people and seen as ungracious.

Present Lost Property can be found in Zones 962-962a. Oddly, this has become a tourist destination in its own right, because it's the only place on the moon where you can see a donkey cork, a talking tennis ball and a tickled onion.

It may surprise you to learn that taking a present home from the moon is not permitted. This upsets most visitors but our laws are made with all good intentions and so it's best not to make a fuss.

What is given on the moon stays on the moon, because we don't want people fighting over things once they have left. It also stops people selling moon things for a vast amount of money, which we think isn't right.

A present is a present and should remain as one. When you leave, there is a sign at the moonport that reads,

'If you take away our presents then you take away our future on your way past.'

It's a message worth thinking about.

Space

Moon people like a bit of space. We also like talking about space. We especially like exploring space.

One space worth exploring is the space in between double-glazing. People look through this space every day but they don't really stop to take a good look inside it.

If they did then they would see it's a fascinating place full of trapped reflections, ribbons of happy bubbles and the ghosts of sand grains. If you look hard enough you might see the colour of the glassmaker's breath and what frame of mind it is in.

There are lots of spaces that get overlooked. The space between two numbers is a remarkable space to explore if you have the time.

For example, if you looked really hard between the numbers 2 and 3 then you would see that there are loads of other numbers living there. There's 2.1, 2.2, 2.3, 2.4, 2.5, 2.6, 2.7, 2.8 and 2.9 to name a few. There's more numbers than that if you look again. You might see 2.11675 playing with 2.11982044 in the rain or you might see 2.561096 playing hopscotch with 2.5555555558 whilst 2.6 looks on wondering when it will get a turn.

We worry about some spaces. We tend to think about the spaces inside a niff-binks head, a hollow pumpkin, a spinal column, and a moon shell. We also worry about the space inside an empty shush-shusha's nest, and the hollow bodies of merry-go round horses.

We spend ages thinking about the spaces between paragraphs, between magic and miracles, between secret and top secret and between a rock and a hard place.

Moon people look at spaces differently to Earth people. You tend to get emotional about car parking spaces whereas we tend to get excited about the space in between magnetic repulsions, the space in between deep breaths, the space between blood bricks and the space in between desperation and inspiration.

Our hearts pump faster thinking about the spaces in between a sniffle and a snuffle, a wobble and a wibble, and a tick and a tock. We get very excited about the space between logs burning on ice fires, the space between toes when they are dancing and the space between friends when they have an argument about peppermints.

You might be wondering why. Well, that's because we think that all space contains something and it is all valuable. We like finding out what the space contains, how it feels and what its plans for the future are.

So much space gets ignored on Earth we find it a bit of a giggle that you want to explore other spaces beyond your scrumptious planet. Our Earth observations show that there are some marvellous spaces just waiting and waiting for a bit of attention.

There are spaces inside lifebuoys, bicycle frames, lamp posts, the blood vessels of bagpipes, statues, envelopes, steel drums, shoe boxes, and threadbare tennis balls. No one gives them a second thought yet these spaces contain life. There might be conversations inside. There might be dreams. There might be an idea waiting to get out.

Sometimes what is inside a space cannot be explained. It can't even be seen. But it's there. You might look inside something and say there is nothing there but that's only because you can't see it or hear it or smell it. Space is packed full of stuff.

We think that some of the most interesting spaces to explore are those where there appears to be no space at all. Tight spaces contain more life than baggy spaces sometimes and they often contain sparks of wonderment.

For example, the space in between the keys of old pianos contain forgotten compositions that someone has played and didn't record; or they contain gossip between musical notes about pianists that didn't make the grade.

A tin of sardines might not grab you as the most exciting place to explore but they contain the blueprints of pilchard projects and the grand designs of sprat missions. These often detail the real intentions of anchovies and why we must always be wary of deep-fried Omega 3.

The space in between the distortions of a jar full of claustrophobic jelly beans is fascinating. If you have a torch you can see what sort of spray they produce and why we shouldn't feel too sorry for them.

Although we find space exploration absorbing there are some spaces we think aren't worth poking around in, such as the space in between hallucinations, or the space in between the toes of hodge-nibs.

We aren't keen on the space inside the interrupted daydreams of cling film or the space under a carpet of lies. They both look the same so watch out.

We recommend that you avoid the space under fingerprint arches and the space under parasite fingernails. They are normally dark, dusty and dangerous places. An abandoned submarine containing a funk virus is a space worth giving a wide berth to and so is the space inside an angry lighthouse with only one cat.

The space inside the wheel of an anxious wheelbarrow should be fine though if you tread carefully. Just check that the wheel was made after 1592 because they were filled with mustard gas before then.

We would highly recommend that you steer clear of the space inside the hollow tonsils of dush gussets. They like to be left alone to meditate about fried grass.

You would imagine that the space in between two slices of fresh bread would be harmless, but try to exercise plenty of caution, because the fillings might not have been prepared by a qualified moon sandwich maker. You might find crockle bugs and faff berries on a spread of rabbit saliva if you are not careful. The space in between this lot is very gummy.

Avoid sandwiches made in the crumb crater where possible as the fillings they use there have been sucked by miggy wigs and then dried out in old sunshine. The space inside a false laugh or an evil laugh isn't worth the hassle but looking inside an endangered laugh most certainly is because you get to see what used to tickle people in ancient times.

It is our humble opinion that we need to explore inner space before we start exploring outer space. That's not to say we shouldn't be interested.

It means that we need to learn as much about our head spaces before we go out into the big wide omniverse making total fools of ourselves.

We are particularly fascinated at the space between people's ears because this seems to be quite vast in some cases.

Whatever you choose to fill your head space with is your business but our advice is to avoid space junk as this tends to clutter the place up and it doesn't help your mind to function to its full potential like ours.

We don't store rubbish in our head spaces like you which is why we have such amazing brains. Rubbish does get into our head space but we empty it three times a day so it doesn't pile up or start to smell. It also stops mind flies from passing on germs and making a nuisance of themselves.

Earth people seem to use their head spaces as dumping grounds which means that things start to rot. If you could see a rotting idea under a mickeyscope then you would see just how unpleasant they are.

Many Earth people bury their head space rubbish underground in their sub-conscious, but a lot of this isn't biodegradable which means it stays there for years. Some Earth people's head space is 90% tripe which leaves very little room for anything else to swim around in. Why fill your head space with bosh, tosh and hogwash when you can fill it with froth, foam and fizzle?!

You Earth people are a funny bunch. Emptying your head of rubbish is a must if you are coming to the moon because we will fill it with wonder and awe if you let us.

As you know, living in the Milky Way suburbs isn't easy because we don't get to see the big picture and the spaces beyond our space. For millennia we have struggled to get to grips with space and understand the universe for what it is and for what it isn't.

Some people used to think that the universe was like a crumpled piece of paper waiting for The Great Puzzler to open it up and flatten it.

Others thought the universe was an elastic band that was being stretched all the time and that if it snapped trillions of other elastic bands would be produced, each one a unique universe.

Many thought that the universe was a phantom that gave birth to new universes each day. Some scientists said that the universe was a piece of ridiculously large film of space snot stretched over a container of galaxies. They believed that if someone picked at the space snot then the galaxies would escape and form their own universes. And then there were those who believed the universe existed in a loop where the past, present and future swapped places with each other, running backwards and forwards trading periods of history with other universes for the highest price.

It's hard to imagine that for gugagillions of years we have known so little about space but what we now know we can share with you.

For example, we know that the universe is one of many universes that sit inside an omniverse of space containers pretty much like a Russian Babushka doll. One universe leads to another for infinity and moon scientists have shown that the smallest spaces contain the largest universes.

We have recently discovered that each universe is different and changes shape according to how it feels. Sometimes this can be thousands of times a day. They inflate and deflate, they turn themselves inside out and back again, they twist and turn, climb and fall.

Scientists once believed that there were one hundred billion galaxies but the latest research shows that this estimate doesn't even scratch the surface of space. We know that one universe alone contains at least this many galaxies, some squiggly, some squidgy and many overlapping like gargantuan Venn diagrams.

Flat galaxies are not dormant as we once believed either. It has come as a shock to know that all galaxies itch, sneeze, scratch, and cough. Even more shocking is the discovery that gravity is not invisible on every planet.

Some galaxies contain super sun solar systems where one giant sun sits in its own space, surrounded by hundreds of solar systems with thousands of planets orbiting around it vying for space. This means that the people on some planets get to see lots of other planets every day, moving from space to place like clouds.

We know a lot more about gunka-galaxies thanks to the Moon-Ogler. This powerful telescope has been able to confirm that gunka-galaxies swallow violent gases, let out screams of x-rays and projectile vomit planets into space. These have been spotted on the edge of the galactic rim moving up and down like space elevators. It is thought that ideas on these planets move at 1.6 million jinkanebs per hour.

The Moon-Ogler has found a remarkable cluster of sleeping galaxies in universe 229. It is estimated that there are 300,000 – 500,000 galaxies that cling together like bats in a space cave.

There are noisy galaxies in some spaces because we can hear them. The Scratch Galaxy produces a continual scraping noise that travels through some parts of space. It sounds like someone running their crunchy fingernails down a blackboard. Scientists think that the scraping is actually produced by space slugs slipping down the side of the galaxy wall.

Space slugs have razor like feet and find it difficult to grip because galaxy walls produce a constant stream of gritty blood cells that stop them holding on for long enough.

We think that people that live on planets in the Scratch Galaxy shout talk. Shout talking is the sort of talk people do when they have got headphones on. They think they are talking at a respectable volume but they are actually speaking louder than they need to. We think that living there would be funny for about five minutes and thereafter it just wouldn't.

We have found all sorts of galaxies by using the moon eye and our 'starchitects' are constantly looking out for other space life. They have spotted migrating galaxies, nocturnal galaxies, fenceless galaxies, sobbing galaxies, kangaroo galaxies and flashback galaxies.

There are galaxies that paddle in shallow space waters and there are galaxies swimming in bottomless space oceans. There are some galaxies that travel vertically and lick the cosmic salt off space cliffs and there are those that hide inside space puddles waiting to be licked by sockfaces.

Some galaxies have a spiritual power that they breathe out. In Universe 17922 the Beatific Galaxy breathes in the toxic gases of the surrounding spaces and breathes out inspiration, gentleness and calm. Space explorers are desperate to reach this part of space but it will be at least 127,000 years before we will be able to get there, unless we can find a spatial short-cut or slip through a hole-less time tunnel.

Galaxies and their parent universes are being discovered all the time. There is the Spinning Tea Cup Galaxy in the T-universe, the Psychedelica Galaxy in Universe 107701 and the Transparent Sponge Galaxy in the Universe of Delusions.

We have recently discovered the Ocean Galaxy where every one of its 500 planets is an ocean planet. We know that all the planets there are at least ten times the size of

Earth and that their oceans are teeming with life just waiting to be discovered.

We know that there is life on every planet because we have detected trillions and trillions of pulses and energy waves. We have no idea how deep the seas are on these giant water planets but we can only assume that they are profound. The discovery of the Ocean Galaxy is even more exciting than finding the Duckweed Galaxy and the twelve sacred rainforest planets.

Some galaxies don't contain any planets or moons at all. Some contain cereal grains, some are saturated in crystals and others are just one big soup of algae waiting for someone to taste them.

In the Dormitory Universe we have plenty of images showing the inside of the Hedgehog Galaxy. Not unsurprisingly it is full of curly ice spikes, barbed wire tendrils, porcupine threats, rose thorns and paralysis hooks. Although the space in between these prickly entities might be worth a look, no one has volunteered yet and an open invitation went out to dozens of solar systems 628 years ago.

In the Twizzle Universe there are millions of galaxies that fall gracefully through space like maple-seed pods. When they appear to hit space ground the twizzle universe turns itself upside down like an egg-timer and the galaxies keep on turning. One of these galaxies has been spotted with a damaged wing membrane and falls erratically. We think it will eventually be rejected by the Twizzle Universe and destroyed.

The biggest know galaxy known to us at the time of writing is the elusive Immortal Galaxy. So many other galaxies want to join up with this galaxy but it seems unlikely that they ever will. The Immortal Galaxy doesn't live in a particular universe. It moves wherever it wants to and never runs out of breath and never tires. It seems to just keep going and going and if anything gets too close for comfort it disappears and pops up in another part of the omniverse.

No one knows what lives inside the Immortal Galaxy because no one can get close enough to it and our telescopes are unable to penetrate its fuzzy skin. We get the feeling that the Immortal Galaxy actually contains some immortal universes in the early stages of their development. These could be nano-eggs waiting to hatch in the right part of space.

One thing that everyone thought they knew about space but didn't, was about its colour. There was no doubt in anyone's mind that space was pitch black and that the only thing that mattered was dark matter. How delightfully wrong centillions of generations were!

Blackness accounts for only 1% of spatial make-up. The other 99% is a profusion of colours beyond our counting capabilities. Some colours have no names because they are so unique we don't know what to call them.

The universes of the omniverse mix new colours all the time and keeping pace with their birth-rate is an impossible task, especially since many of these are ultra-violet colours which many Earth people cannot see. However, we can forgive ourselves for thinking that space was just a black vastness because we live in black space and have been kept in the dark until now.

After many years studying space from the moon's surface we have learnt that you cannot make space or create space. It creates you. You are space and you always will be. Our space is your space and you are welcome to share it with us for a while although terms and conditions apply.

GETTING TO THE MOON

You might be wondering how you get to the moon in the first place. Well, although we are only 29 bingabungs away, Earth technology cannot reach us that quickly yet.

There are three main travel options open to you, and it's worth considering each one carefully before making a total fool of yourself.

The TeleMoon Express

One option is the TeleMoon Express. This is a teletransporter that works by scanning your brain and body cells and then destroying them. The information scanned is then beamed to the moon and you are reconstructed in our moon ports. It's a bit like scanning a bar code of your DNA and e-mailing it.

Although the person on the moon looks, feels and thinks the same as the person who has just been scanned on Earth, you are essentially a new person. You basically walk into a teleport bay on Earth, go to sleep and wake up on the moon about ten minutes later.

This is by far the fastest way of getting to the moon, and is chosen by a lot of people, but it isn't for everyone. You see, teletransporting only claims to be 99% safe.

This means there is a 1% chance of something not going according to plan. Although the TeleMoon Express Company doesn't hide this fact, they don't make a meal of it, either, because they would go out of business otherwise.

Many Earth people are aware of the risks, but turn a blind eye to them because teletransporting is so quick – ten minutes is hardly a lifetime. Compare this to 18 hours by moon tube and 2 days by moon bus.

But let's not overlook the risks of teletransporting. The most common side-effect is a bad reaction to scanning. Some people don't wake up straight away and can spend a week asleep. You can imagine how this would severely disrupt a family holiday.

Another problem encountered is waking up on the moon and feeling like feet fish are nibbling your toes. This can last for about two days and isn't pleasant, because you spend most of that time looking down and saying, 'Get off!'

Another side-effect to scanning is waking up demanding to go home. This again severely disrupts a family holiday. People that wake up in this state cannot be talked into staying, as they start to become rude and go blue in the face. They are quickly transported back. The only other side-effects that have been reported are warm fingers, a bruised ego, and a loss of appetite.

The least reported problem is being scanned and beamed, but not actually making it to the moon. It has been known for the data being sent to disappear into a megadata cloud. These are dense black blobs of sticky information that move from space to space, hoping to capture any information that is being transmitted.

A megadata cloud basically trips the data up as it travels, scrambles it, and then covers it in a virtual code-slime so that it is unusable and unreadable. The data is unable to move and it is impossible to retrieve it as it is mixed with other pieces of sticky data. We don't think that megadata clouds do anything with the data beyond that. They seem to just collect information, although some scientists think the data is being slowly digested over several million years.

We estimate that a typical cloud measuring 100 miles wide holds as much as 50 million internet systems from different planets. Despite their enormity, megadata clouds are notoriously difficult to detect. We think they fall through trapdoors and plop out the other side in a different part of the omniverse, capturing even more data. We have no idea how many trapdoors there are in our solar system, because we don't know what they look like and no one has ever seen one.

The Moon Bus

The moon bus is probably the safest way of travelling to the moon, but it is also the slowest. Moon buses are capable of carrying about 1,000 people at a time, which is impressive, but this makes getting on one a problem. In fact, by the time everyone's luggage has been searched and people have been interviewed about their travel plans, you can easily add another 24 hours on top of your total travel experience. You will be pleased to know that checking into the moon is much more efficient, and we can process 1,000 people in under an hour.

Moon buses are generally pretty cramped, and they can get a bit claustrophobic but they are reliable and they have never broken down. Putting these things aside, moon buses can boast of giving you some of the best views of Earth you will ever have. This is because the roof of a moon bus peels back to reveal a hyper-toughened glass ceiling. This is your window into space, and the views are spectacular. The roof folds back as you approach the moon.

There are plans to build a 2,000-seater moon bus with a transparent floor, and this should be ready by the end of the decade. At the moment, there are only five moon buses in operation from Earth.

The Moon Tube

The third option is the moon tube – a 225,000-mile elevator that will take you from Earth's doorstep to our doorstep in less than an Earth day. This amazing lift can accommodate about 100 people at a time. Don't worry – you don't have to stand up. The lift is like a three-storey house where passengers sit upstairs; luggage goes in the middle and the crew work on the ground floor.

The moon tube is very popular, but there is only one. It is built on an island in the Indian Ocean, and not everyone can reach it easily. It took almost 59 years to build and 'cost the Earth' to build, as some Earth people have told us.

Travelling on the moon tube is a smooth experience, but it doesn't have any windows, so it can be boring. However, it is safe and there has only ever been one incident when the power failed for a few minutes. No one was injured and the lift did not crash back down to Earth, as some people thought it might. It just scared everyone senseless.

The most expensive route here is by TeleMoon Express. The moon bus is the cheapest and the moon tube is in the middle. The waiting lists for travelling by either moon bus or moon tube are enormous, because of limited space. This isn't a problem for teletransporting. What is a problem, though, is that the moon restricts the number of visitors per month, otherwise we would be overpopulated and overcooked very quickly.

We are such an exciting destination and very popular with Earth people wanting to celebrate their honeymoon here. We sometimes wish we had a twin. Some moon scientists think we do have a twin.

What really annoys us is that rich Earth people with their own moon buses seem to think they have the right to just turn up whenever they like. We might be friendly, but we don't like that sort of attitude.

They offer us money and lots of it to let them land, but what they forget is that money is worthless on the moon. We banned money after seeing all the problems it caused on Earth. No, anyone turning up on a whim is denied entry and escorted back by our sky police. There are no exceptions. On the moon, everyone is treated equally, and we mean it.

We have no problem with people visiting the space around us though. Lots of people with their own moon buses fly around the moon and look at us from a distance. That's fine.

Space Hazards

However, if you are travelling in space using your own moon bus, then you may need to know a few things about the hazards involved, especially if it's your first time. The thing is, space travel is risky.

You might fly 1,000 times and never have a problem. Then again, you might fly once and regret it for the rest of your life. You see, it's not uncommon to disappear.

There are four main things to be aware of, and beware of at all times: space tears, space holes, space webs and space curtains. These are invisible and impossible to spot or detect (to us), so this makes things space travel exciting, perilous and crazy.

A space tear is exactly what it says – a slit in space. The tear is like a cut, but without the blood and plaster. So there you all are, flying happily along one second, and you're gone the next. That's because you have slipped through a flap of space skin and ended up someplace else. This could be on the other side of space. Where this is, no one knows, because we don't know how many sides space really has.

You could be on the inside of space or the outside of space. You might even be inside the outside of space or outside the inside. You might find yourself in an awkward space or the space might be inside someone's head.

Now, this could be good news if you end up in the mindspace of a savant. Their brains are so big, they are like mini-universes themselves, packed with mesmerising ideas, dreams and adventures. If you end up in the mindspace of a space goat, though, that would be bad news. Although the space inside is vast, there's nothing to see or do there.

If you slip through a tear in space, then it's difficult to say how long you'll be gone for, because time moves forwards, backwards and sideways in space. It also twists, turns, spins, stands still, and evaporates. This is hard to understand if you are used to time moving in circles and dates moving along timelines. In some parts of the omniverse, time repeats itself in a loop every 60 seconds.

Most people fear slipping through a space tear because they think they will never see their families and friends again. There is no need to fret, though, because you always end up where you started ... eventually.

When you do return, you have no memory of where you have been and no one has missed you. This is a good thing, because if you have had a dreadful experience you'd rather forget, then having no memory of it in the first place saves a lot of bother.

We have to say that slipping through a space tear is better than falling down a space hole.

If you happen to fall into a hole in space, chances are you'll be lost for good. Space holes connect to tunnels and tunnels join onto other tunnels. There are tunnels galore in space; infinite tunnels, in fact. Tunnels have a habit of losing anything that falls into them. This isn't deliberate, it's just that tunnels are forgetful: they have no sense of direction; none of the tunnels have names and they move so quickly, they can't keep up with themselves.

Space webs aren't nice. There are space spiders that travel across the fabric of space spinning web traps. You can't see them, but they are there, waiting. Space spiders always work in pairs. They may be related, but we aren't sure. Together, they spin enormous webs, with the intention of catching anything that can think.

We believe that space craft get caught in these webs like flies and just sit there in space, waiting for the inevitable. Space spiders enjoy the wait, because they know that once anything is in their web, escape is impossible.

Last but not least, we need to warn you about space curtains. These are no ordinary curtains, although they behave in the same way as normal curtains do.

Space curtains measure at least 500 million km wide and have a drop of 2,000 million km. We have been told that they are like enormous stage curtains that open and close with a flourish, and that they get quite excited when they sense an approaching space vessel in their space. Pilots have to be especially skilful to avoid them, as they cannot be seen until the last minute, by which time it's normally too late.

The curtains open at breakneck speed and suck you in. If you are unlucky enough to fly through some space curtains and they close behind you, it quite literally spells 'curtains' for you and your fellow travellers. All those that enter the curtains are never seen again, unless of course, the curtains fail to close.

Despite the dangers of space tears, space holes, space webs and space curtains, many Earth people risk everything to get a closer look at the moon. Look into the sky from the moon and you'll often see half a dozen private moon buses passing by.

Whichever way you get to the moon, we know that once you are here, you won't want to leave. Before you leave Earth, remember to have a full brain scan and e-mail this to us so that we check your thinking and make sure that you are not importing harmful ideas into the moon's atmosphere. Without a brain scan, you will not be allowed to travel. You will also need to drink at least 14 litres of water before a trip, as space travel is dehydrating.

Other moon words of interest

There are lots of words that have a moon connection. Here are a few of them. Our comments appear in italics.

Atlantic Moonfish – fishes with very flat bodies.
It doesn't sound like there is much meat on them.

Full-Moon Maple – a small, graceful tree from Japan.
Sounds lovely.

Honeymoon – a holiday taken by a newly married couple immediately after their wedding.
Bees could be a problem.

Mock Moon – a lunar halo.
We like the idea of having one of those.

Moonbeam – a ray of light from the moon.
We are always beaming on the moon.

Moonblindness – a term for night blindness.
We don't get this because of our infra-red vision.

Moonstomp – a dance with heavy stamping.
We like a good stomp.

Moonwalk – a backslide dance technique that gives the illusion of being pulled forward while attempting to walk forward.

We do this when no one is looking.

Moon Child – someone born under the sign of Cancer.
*That has to be better than being born under the sign
'Emergency Exit'.*

Moon Face – having a very round face.
Nothing wrong with that.

Mooning – to expose your bottom for all to see.
Plenty wrong with that.

Moonglade – the bright reflection of the moon's light on
an expanse of water.
Delightful.

Moonpie – a type of cake consisting of two round
crackers with a marshmellow filling dipped in chocolate.
Put us down for a couple hundred dozen.

Moonraker – someone who pretends to be a simpleton.
Some don't need to pretend.

Moonrat – a hedgehog.
They sound like trouble.

Mooneye – a small fish found in the waters of North
America.
Groovy. Do they sing?

Moonbow – this is a rainbow produced by light reflected
off the surface of the moon rather than by direct sunlight.
It is also known as a lunar rainbow or a white rainbow.
There are no arrows involved.

Moonrise – the rising of the moon above the horizon.
We rise, you shine.

Moonsail – a sail sometimes carried in light winds above a skysail.
We've seen one for sale but had second thoughts.

Moonseed – a poisonous climbing plant that resembles a crescent moon.
They aren't welcome on the moon.

50 THINGS YOU DIDN'T KNOW ABOUT THE MOON

Getting to know things about moon people and life on the moon will help you make the most of your visit. For example, did you know that moon caterpillars are afraid of curtains? Did you know that moon people don't trust socks? And did you know that a moon owl can twit but not twooo? Here are just some of the things you should know:

1. A starving moon sentence will eat its own words to stay alive.
2. Dinner plates on the moon have mouths on them. They eat anything you leave and will lick themselves clean.
3. Moon people are always losing their voices. They tend to hide in cracks, under rocks or under carpets.
4. Large seagulls with oxygen tanks strapped to their backs can be found flying above Crater 452.
5. Moon cats have one eye that is yellow and another eye that is green, red or transparent.
6. Zebra crossings on the moon have flashing white stripes.
7. Some things float on the moon. Some things sink. Some do neither.
8. A lot of the moon's electrical power comes from vegetables.

9. The moon orbits the Earth but the hemispheres of the moon rotate in different directions.
10. Moon trees bark. So do moon squirrels.
11. Some moon people will hold their chins with their left hands, because they are worried their heads will roll off.
12. Moon people love eating oranges. They also like eating yellows, reds and browns, but not greens.
13. The head of a nail contains very little oxygen.
14. Moon sand traps can swallow themselves.
15. Moon mirrors are expensive and come with a bad luck guarantee of 700 years if cracked and 4900 years if smashed.
16. The bunkum bird was made extinct 50 years before it was born to save time.
17. A moonslide of tumbling polyhedrons killed 198 moon echoes in 1432.
18. The moon has colossal natural resources and is the solar system's largest exporter of ideas and dreams.
19. 85% of moon people can tie shoelaces with one hand. The other 15% wishes they could.
20. It is illegal to talk to doors on the moon.
21. Moon water is purified in the reflection of moon mirrors.
22. Moon people all share the same DNA, but everyone has a different tongue-print.
23. Crater 30 is 21,000km wide and 12km deep. It is home to the magical moonfish.
24. Vegetables on the moon can scream.
25. One of the best-selling chocolate bars on the moon is called Plop-Plop.
26. Moon robots get arthritis in the shoulder but nowhere else.

27. All moon people can write with one hand and draw with the other.
28. Moon people like jumping through cobwebs and feathers.
29. Every moon puddle tells a story…literally!
30. Every day on the moon is a Monday. Every day on the moon is also a bad hair day.
31. There is a café on the moon called T-Minus 10.
32. The distance a moon cow's moo travels is used as a unit of measurement on the moon.
33. The force of a moon brainwave is enough to lift 500 elephants off the ground.
34. Moon people are born with six toes on their left foot and seven on their right.
35. The lunar floor bounces like a drum skin every 55 minutes.
36. Moon spiders hear through their eyes.
37. One of the most popular games on the moon is cube chasing.
38. There is a hotel in Crater Croaker in the shape of a Martian elephant. The hotel has its reception area in its bottom, accessed via a ladder.
39. Stepping-stones on the moon are psychic.
40. There are 336 moons in the solar system.
41. Moon women are born with two hearts and men with only one.
42. The oldest piece of chewing gum in the solar system can be found on the moon.
43. Miracle bags that don't work have holes in them and all the magic leaks out.
44. Smelling moon oranges helps you lose weight.
45. If moon people want to make their hair stick up they use bisk dung.

46. Moon shadows can cast shadows of their own.
47. The moon used to be covered in a layer of quint, a sort of gritty purple oil that belched.
48. You weigh more at the Equator than you do at the Poles of the moon.
49. A moon goldfish has a memory of 300 years.
50. The moon has gravity hotspots. Gravity in Zones 45-90 is stronger than anywhere else on the moon. If gravity is strong it slows down the ageing process, which is why most people want to move to this part of the moon.

FREQUENTLY ASKED QUESTIONS ABOUT THE MOON

People ask a lot of questions about the moon. Some of these get asked frequently enough to deserve the title FAQ.

To qualify as a FAQ, a question has to be asked enough times to get on someone else's nerves.

We have collected some FAQs together so we don't run out of breath, run out of patience, or get bored.

We have included answers from a variety of moon people and so it is for you to decide what to believe. Some may be right and others may just be a lot of moonwash and moonhoggle.

1. When did the first Earth people land on the moon?

Not in 1969, as many think. The Fram people of the ancient North Pole were the first here over 4,000 years ago, but Earth people have no record of this.

The Frams were the most advanced people of their time and sent 300 people here in one trip on their craft Axis 1. The second ice age wiped out the Fram civilisation and all their remarkable breakthroughs. It is believed that their mega-cities are frozen in time under what is now Greenland.

2. Is it true that the moon is a speck of pollen that has blown from Flower Galaxy 2?

We don't think so, but if it were, it would explain all the sneezing that goes on here.

3. What if the moon fell down?

We would keep falling through space until we hit some space skin. This would bounce us back to where we started. The moon has fallen out of Earth's gravity six times in the last two billion years, and we fully expect it to happen again in the next million years or so. Let's hope so because we love trampolining!

4. What is the moon made of?

The moon is made up of many layers. The outer layer is a gunpowdery dust called jollop. Then there is the outer inner layer, made up of tightly packed consonants. Beneath this is the outer inner internal layer, which is mostly space straw.

Next is the outer inner internal interior layer, stuffed full of rope knots covered in a superglue paste of moon-dog saliva.

Inside the outer inner internal interior is the innermost middle, where you will find a ball of pleasantly warm water, home to millions of bioluminescent fish with diamonds for scales. Floating somewhere inside the moon sea is a rhombicosidodecahedron. This contains at least 10,000 moon secrets.

5. What shape is the moon?

Well, it's not a circle. It's not spherical, either. It's egg-shaped – another way of saying that is *ovoid*. The moon changes into one of five shapes every 500 million years: a cube, a cuboid, a prism, a pyramid or an ovoid.

It has been an ovoid for the last 300 million years, and in 200 million years, it will turn back into a cube again. We think that in a billion years, we won't have a shape; we will just have style.

6. How long does it take for the moon to go round the Earth?

This depends what mood we are in. I suppose the approximate time taken is about 27 days. If you want to be exact, and many people like to be, it takes 27 days, 7 hours, 43 minutes, 11.6 seconds. Well, it is if you follow the 24-hour clock. For those tourists visiting us from Mars, it takes the moon 459 glips, 7,900 bon-bons and -9 zims to dance around the Earth.

7. Is the moon a planet?

Tough one. Pluto used to be classified as a planet by people on Earth. The moon is bigger than Pluto, so I suppose we could be called a planet. Then people on Earth changed their minds and decided Pluto wasn't a planet, so I suppose we aren't really a planet, either.

We are often called 'out of this world' by visitors, though. Moon people have applied to The Interplanetary Astro Union to be upgraded to a dwarf planet. We haven't heard anything yet and we wonder whether anyone bothered to put a stamp on the envelope.

8. Has there ever been an Olympic Games on the moon?

Yes, sort of: we were hosts for the 2080 Solar System Games, which was a huge success. The records for the long jump, side jump, high jump and wide jump were all smashed. A new solar system record for throwing a wobbler was set at 1,048m by our own athlete Stella Mahoonahoon.

9. Are there any seas on the moon?

Yes. We recommend that you visit the Sea of Serenity and the Sea of Crises in the north and the Sea of Nectar and the Sea of Moisture in the south. Some of our seas are underground, and not visible from Earth or from the surface of the moon. Some are frozen and some are angry, but we don't know much more about them. In fact, we know more about deep space than we do about our own deep seas.

10. What happened to the footprints Neil Armstrong made in 1969?

They actually walked away to explore the moon themselves after Mr Armstrong and his friends went home. The footprints eventually got stuck in some jinkle snut and there they stayed until the Moon Museum was built around them.

The footprints should last for 10 million years at least, so long as the jinkle snut doesn't break apart. The first footprint by Mr Armstrong was made by his left foot and it is customary therefore to step into the museum with your left foot first. Not the right. Just remember that left is right and right is wrong.

11. Is it true that Buzz Aldrin's mum was called Moon before she was married?

Yes, before becoming Mrs Marion Aldrin, her maiden name was Marion Moon. Buzz Aldrin was the second person to walk on the moon. Some people think he should have been the first human from Earth to step on us, given that he has moon in his blood. We are pleased he came, though, as there has been a buzz around the place ever since.

12. How much would a piece of lunar cheesecake cost me on the moon?

If you get to the moon in one piece, then you get your first piece of lunar cheesecake on the house. After that, it depends what you can trade in return. Moon people like to learn something new, so if you can tell them something they don't know already, you might get a piece with your name on it.

13. How common is theft on the moon?

We are proud to say that our own moon citizens do not commit crime. However, space tourists, including astronauts, are fond of taking moon rocks as souvenirs. This is widely frowned upon and totally prohibited. Over 100,000kg of moon rock has been stolen since we opened our doors to tourists.

14. How wide is the largest crater on the moon?

144 miles long. This houses the moon MegaCity of Zirna. We recommend you try the plastic moon cakes and the deep-focus coffee there.

15. Can you see the Great Wall of China from the moon?

No.

16. Does the moon vibrate?

Yes, every 55 minutes, the lunar surface vibrates for 60 seconds. The vibrations aren't life-threatening, so don't worry. They are gentle, and many moon people take off their shoes for a foot massage.

17. Is the moon masculine or feminine?

The moon is the moon and it is what it is.

18. Is it true that there is a crater full of old 'delete' buttons from Earth computer keyboards?

Yes, although the crater isn't full anymore. Earth people agreed that after dismantling old computer keyboards, each separate key would be shipped to a different part of the solar system for recycling. We agreed to accept all the delete buttons and the Pidge-wickers have been feeding on these for the last two years.

Pidge-wickers are bald, sausage-like creatures about 15 inches long that feed only on the 4th, 5th, 12th and 20th letters of an alphabet, which is why delete buttons are the perfect source of energy. The RRR Crater probably only has about 1,780 tons of delete buttons left.

19. Is the water safe to drink on the moon?

Moon water passes through at least 100 filter fish before being washed in moon mirror reflections. It will then travel around purification pipes for three days before being blessed by a magical wishing fish. The wish water you drink is 100% safe and is suitable for washing everything except jeans, genes and shoes made of ostrich tongue. You can drink the water straight from the Lake of Dreams, too.

20. Are maggots a problem on the moon?

They used to be. For a short time in our history, moon maggots would congregate on the street corners of most craters, spitting biscuit crumbs at tourists, but they have gone now. Please don't worry about them.

21. Are immunisations needed for moon travel?

We recommend having a jab to help prevent moon wobble, a jab for word rock to avoid mid-sentence anxiety attacks and a jab for helping reduce the effect of air-jibbles.

When travelling to a rainbow crater, you will need a certificate to show that you have been vaccinated against kaleidoscope fever, especially if you are coming from an area infected with cracked mirrors and broken reflections.

22. Can I take photographs on the moon?

Taking mental photographs are fine but always ask permission of moon people first if you want to look at them for longer than 10 seconds whilst you focus.

23. Is tipping accepted on the moon, and how much should I tip?

We don't like pollution of any kind, so tipping is not allowed.

24. How is the nightlife on the moon?

It's the same as the light life but dark.

25. Any advice on shopping?

No, not really. Just don't shop after drinking a Brussels sprout and black cabbage milkshake.

QNATO ABOUT THE MOON

Questions Not Asked That Often about the moon have not yet been asked enough times to be promoted to FAQ status. A sample of QNATO can be found here:

1. What types of plugs can I use on the moon?

Ear plugs are probably best if you are a light sleeper. You can also wear bath plugs around your neck in some craters.

2. What happens if I have a complaint to make?

Keep it to yourself. Try rubbing some cream into it.

3. Do I need to avoid moonquakes?

No. They will probably avoid you though, if your smell is unfamiliar.

4. What do you recommend I pack in my pencil-case?

Midge-nippers will come in handy and so will some colourless crayons.

5. How far away is the moon?

That depends where you are coming from and whether you get lost. It will also depend on whether your legs contain a lot of magnetism.

6. How wide is the moon?

Wide. It is about 83 stomps or 2098 shilly-clongs. Why does no one ask us how tall we are?

7. Is chewing gum banned on the moon?

Yes, it is, although there is a band in the Ziggy Crater called Chewing Gum. Some people who have heard their music think they should be banned, too.

8. Is it true that you can feast on sore eyes on the moon?

Yes, moon people's eyes are detachable and eyes that become sore are often taken out and fried with onions and peppers. Some restaurants will serve sore eyes with moon pigeon brains and gug liver.

9. Is rhubarb popular on the moon?

It is if you have the stomach for it. Rhubarb grown on the moon is ten times stronger than that on Earth and it is a powerful laxative.

Many tourists have regretted eating our rhubarb crumbles. Eating moon rhubarb can also make you twitch and it has been known to send some people floppy.

10. Can you hold your breath on the moon?

No. It's too slippy and it just runs through your fingers.

11. Does the moon have any oil reserves?

No, but scientists have recently discovered that the moon contains vast amounts of adrenaline in the Northern

Hemisphere under the Bay of Rainbows, which we hope to start drilling soon. We plan to give this to lethargic moon cows and listless moon snails.

12. Is a stamp necessary for posting a letter home?

No, a stamp won't get you very far. A skip or a run to the letterbox would be better. Walking is fine.

13. Have the Slug Wars ended now?

The Slug Wars never really started. A field of slugs from the Hoop Crater declared war on a field of slugs in the Ghost Tip Crater. They made friends before any fighting began. They have all now been eaten.

14. Does the moon have any beaches?

Yes, it does. There are lots of them and there are two types.

You will find mirror beaches and petal beaches. Mirror beaches are covered in soft reflective flakes of space skin the size of thumbnails. This gives the illusion of walking on a mirror. Look down and you will see what's up.

Petal beaches are covered in the petals of flower heads dropped by toozin birds. These industrious birds pick fresh flowers from the fields along the moon belt all day and night. These beaches are particularly sweet-smelling and very soft underfoot.

15. Do circles get dizzy on the moon?

Circles by definition go round and round, but the strength of gravity on the moon combined with antidizzle tablets dissolved into a circle's circumference means that our circles never get dizzy.

16. Is there room to swing a cat on the moon?

We banned this over 600 years ago. You can, however, see swinging cats in the Moondish Circus who work as trapeze artists.

17. Can moon people keep a secret?

Moon people like to keep all sorts of things, especially something that doesn't need a walk three times a day or taking to the vets every 5 minutes. So yes, secrets are fine, because they don't wee on the carpet.

18. Does the moon reflect anything else other than sunlight?

Yes, we reflect a lot of ambition and a lot of dreams. We also reflect a lot on questions we don't know the answer to. We tend to absorb criticism and sweat endeavour. We often fire bolts of inspiration from the lighthouses of the Northern and Southern Tiptops.

19. Is it true what they say about moon apples?

Yes – if you bite into one, you will taste orange. Moon oranges taste of apples.

20. Are barbecues allowed on the moon?

The only barbecues we allow are alphabet barbecues, and all letters must be thoroughly cooked to avoid word poisoning.

21. What will you find at the foot of a moon mountain?

You will probably find lots of shoes. All the old shoes that moon people don't want any more are buried at the feet of moon mountains as a mark of respect.

22. Do I need to bring a toothbrush and toothpaste?

There is no need to. We have mouth worms that clean our teeth and they make a brilliant job of it, too. These clever creatures secrete fluoride and baking soda as they move up and down and from side to side in our mouths. When they have done, we spit them out. You can swallow them, too.

23. Is there anywhere to play golf on the moon?

Yes, the Terraced Trap Crater is home to 12 different courses and has been described by some enthusiasts as 'golfing heaven'. Each course is a different colour and with a different number of holes.

24. Can I bring a pet to the moon?

No pets. You can, however, bring a carpet, a trumpet or a puppet.

25. What can I do if I get bored on the moon?

On the moon, boredom is impossible.

Lightning Source UK Ltd.
Milton Keynes UK
174372UK00001B/3/P